Doorways to Freedom

Truths Fantastically Told

AF200331

Bernd Strohmeyer

Doorways to Freedom

Truths Fantastically Told

Illustrated by

Marah Strohmeyer-Haider

© 2017 Bernd Strohmeyer

Illustrations © 2017 Marah Strohmeyer-Haider Production and publication:

BoD - Books on Demand, Norderstedt, GERMANY

ISBN 9783748107361

TABLE OF CONTENTS

Foreword

In the beginning is longing.

It is longing that drives us, gives us strength, encourages us to go looking for things in life. Having no idea what we are looking for, we set off without any aim or direction to begin with, on our heroic emotional journey. Battles with anxiety, trust, challenges, successes, resistances, walls, love, hurt, happiness... all these have to be gone through, and with each new experience we get a little bit closer to ourselves. We understand better and better who we are, what we need and what makes us different. However, we don't reach the goal, because as time passes not only external things change – we ourselves change as well. As our taste in food changes from childhood to old age, so too with our taste for life. We come across foods that are unusual, but fascinating in their strangeness; sense impressions which, once you have experienced them, you wouldn't want ever to be without. What ingredients influence our feeling for life? What new things have been added? What has changed? What might we still develop a liking for?

This book is designed to give you a few suggestions. Life issues are presented in a dreamy and playful way, in a colorful mixture of short stories, fables, fairy tales and parables. The stories are doorways which open up different points of view, direct the reader's attention in unknown directions and offer a new kind of taste for life. Multilayered works of art by my dear wife give further insights into what lies behind them.

During my training in humanistic and systemic therapy methods, the writing of stories was a quite personal way for me to adapt my insights and make them more tangible. The stories were companions along my path of personal development, and helped me to establish new patterns of thinking. I did not think of publication at the time. Later on I let myself to be persuaded to make these ideas accessible to others. Here my wife, with her wonderful gift for expressing in pictures what cannot be stated in words, has encouraged, supported and complemented me.

We invite you to wonder, to let yourself be driven by fantastical truths, to plunge into the depths of the pictures and walk through the doorways into freedom.

Bernd Strohmeyer

Meditation

I stand on the beach
and look out to sea.
The sea is life.
It is so very beautiful.

I gaze at the horizon and run laughing into the water,
into the gentle pain of the cold.
The wetness washes round my legs, deepens,
till I dare to leap.

My breath stands still, my heart beats wildly,
soft touch embraces me
with the feeling of invigoration.

Life with its heaviness makes me lighter.
It carries me over dark abysses.
Out of the depths rise beasts, plants, other persons.
A world of sensations
which make me forget
where I come from.

But I must come up for air,
need new breath, new energy,
lift my head out of the water,
over life,
into the stillness.

Here I can draw new breath,
can see the sea,
can see my life,
can look into my dying,
then plunge in again,
until I return to the beach.

I stand on the beach
and look out to sea.
The sea is life.
It is so very beautiful.

Alone

Under a spruce in the Alps there stands a gigantic anthill. The anthill has been there for a long time. The ant people who have built the hill and maintain it now add up to many millions.

This is the story of a small, perfectly insignificant ant. To be precise, a worker ant named Bernd.

Bernd has had a pretty long life, and has always worked hard and conscientiously in fulfilling his tasks – looking after fungus cultures, extending galleries, carrying plants and dead creatures into the anthill and so on. Often, and indeed very often in recent times, Bernd talks to other ants about the world, the dangers outside the anthill and the meaning of life. He listens to the tales and experiences of the other ants respectfully and with curiosity. Sometimes he wonders whether he too would like to have such adventures. "Well, it's fascinating somehow… but a bit scary." So time passes. Bernd can't let go of his curiosity or his questions about the world.

It's night, the other ants have gone to sleep. Bernd resolves to do something he has never done before. He leaves the complex, goes to the spruce which stands next to the anthill and climbs to the very top of the tree. From here he sees, for the first time in his life, the surrounding mountains, the wide landscape and the bright starry sky in all its glory. It suddenly becomes clear to him how big the world is, how infinitely various the universe and how small he himself is. He's just a little ant that may be trodden on at any time, may be eaten at any time, one that can even drown in a drop of rain. Nobody would know. He is much too small to be noticed. It would be just a simple, aimless, random occurrence.

Bernd senses a great loneliness. A loneliness that is just as big and cold as the universe – an infinite loneliness.

He goes back to his friends and tells them about his feelings of loneliness. They react incredulously. "You are part of a vast and perfectly organized society. You are our friend! We love you! How can you be lonely?" they say. Bernd can't make sense of it himself. He does love his friends. He is happy to be part of the tribe. But all the same… this feeling won't go away. On the contrary, the more of his fellows are around, the stronger the sense of loneliness.

Bernd decides to leave the anthill to look for a medicine for loneliness.

He packs a big backpack – ants can carry a hundred times their own body weight – and marches south, following the sun. After a few hours' march, he climbs on a blade of grass to look around. "O dear, I can still see the anthill on the horizon. How can I find anything that will help me, when I'm still so near to home?"

Vroom! An ibex races over the grass blade. Bernd is just able to hang onto its fleece. Now they progress at rapid speed over hill and down dale. Breathlessly the ibex charges into a cliff face and climbs with agility to the top of a mountain peak. Here Bernd drops off, praying fervently that the beast won't trample on him.

But he's in luck. The ibex goes its way and nothing happens.

When the starry night comes on, the band of the Milky Way enshrouds the empty infinity of the universe. Bernd now feels worse than lonely, he feels quite abandoned. "That now is the entire truth," he thinks, and cries himself to sleep.

Is it a dream or is it a miracle? He sees a star in the Milky Way coming towards him. The point of light comes closer and closer, becomes bigger and brighter. As his eyes habituate to the brightness, he can see a tiny, pretty fairy at the heart of the light. She circles around Bernd a few times, titters quietly and finally says: "Well, you are a funny little guy. You look SO ugly with your feelers and your big multifaceted eyes. Shouldn't you be sitting in an anthill and working, along with the rest of your kind?" When Bernd hears her say this, he thinks, "She's right" – and he starts to sob gently. "Whoa!" exclaims the little fairy. "You really are a sensitive soul. I only wanted to provoke you a bit, so you would try to catch me. Let's have a game."

"I really don't feel like playing games," says Bernd. "I am on a long and very dangerous quest." – "Yikes!" the fairy exclaims. Her little wings flutter with excitement. "That sounds incredibly exciting. So what are you looking for?" – "A medicine for loneliness," Bernd answers. The fairy looks completely nonplussed, forgets to beat her wings and lands awkwardly on the ground. "Wow, you really got me there," she says. "Do you really believe that there is such a thing? Sometimes I could do with a medicine like that. I'm so small that the other fairies hardly pay any attention to me. When they fly away, I can't keep up with them. I'm always the last, and I don't want to go on being treated like a fifth wheel. So I just took off. They won't miss me anyway. But being so alone in the world makes you feel very lonely. I don't care so much any more about your being ugly. I want this medicine too."

"Can this really turn out well?" Bernd wonders. "We could hardly be any more different. Every day she'll be telling me how ugly and twisted I am. Well, of course a beautiful fairy is going go see an ant as a monster. Is this really what I want? Beauty and the Beast? But then again, she's not happy either, and together we might have a better chance of finding something."

"Okay," Bernd says. – "Yippee!" cries the fairy, and lands beaming on Bernd's back. "That way," she calls, pointing to the horizon as she hops excitedly. Bernd just shakes his head. For the first time, he's got to come up with a plan.

The ill assorted couple have now been moving for two hours toward the rising sun. That is, Bernd walks and the fairy sits petulantly on his back. This wasn't what she was expecting. A distance that she covers in flight in the space of five minutes takes Bernd a whole hour. He has to circumnavigate every grass blade, clamber over every stone, every pile of earth must be painfully surmounted or else avoided by going the long way round. From the fairy's point of view, this is all perfectly crazy. "How could the creation ever have brought forth such a slow, laborious and vulnerable creature as an ant?" the fairy complains. She hasn't used the word "ugly" this time, but Bernd again feels extremely lonely. Back home, he never felt that he was slow. Well, in races he was no better than average, but when it came to weight lifting he was always proud of his performance. But now…

"I'll have to do something," says the fairy. "We're not getting anywhere. This way we will never find the medicine." The fairy flies off, leaving Bernd waiting despondently.

"If only I were a fairy," Bernd thinks. "Then I could fly, I wouldn't have to be scared of getting squashed, I would be pretty and everything would be straight and simple. Yes… ants do maintain the ecosystem in the woods, keep the pests down, protect plants and all that. But to be a fairy – that would be fantastic! – What jobs do fairies do actually? I must ask her sometime."

The fairy only gets back late in the evening. She's accompanied by a very ancient, totally shriveled fairy who looks more like a moth or some kind of insect. "This is Void," the fairy says. "Void is a medicine man and the spiritual leader of the fairies. You wouldn't believe the trouble I had persuading them to let me come back. And it was a lengthy struggle getting Void to come with me. But I'll tell you all about it another time."

Void takes up a position in front of Bernd and the fairy. He stands quite still and looks at both of them searchingly. Then he asks, in quiet but firm tones, "What do you need?" Bernd tells him his story, that he is looking for a medicine for loneliness, that the fairy wanted to help him, that he was much too slow and didn't know how to recognize the medicine even if he found it, and he hardly has any hope left of ever finding it. Void listens carefully without moving a muscle.

After a pause, he says, "Loneliness depends on the breadth of your perceptions, and on your definition of who and what you are. You have extended your perceptions. Now it's time for you to extend yourself."

He fumbles with a small bag he is holding, and throws the contents of the bag over Bernd's back. The burning sensation and the itching makes Bernd convulse. He feels faint and passes out.

When he wakes up, the fairy is holding him in her arms and stroking his head. Something feels totally different. But what is it? He looks into the fairy's eyes, which flash at him expectantly. His back isn't hurting now, but there's something attached to it. He turns round, to see and… "Wings! I've got wings!" cries Bernd. Bernd and the fairy jump up and do a dance to celebrate.

The rest of the evening passes merrily. Bernd's first flying attempts, in the dark and with the fairy assisting, generally end in a thicket or collision with a tree trunk – at all events with some kind of discomfiture. However, never mind, Bernd is thrilled to be flying, so he doesn't mind the scrapes and the bruises. And he's getting better with every attempt.

Next morning, the odd couple stand on a hill and gaze happily over the wide landscape extending to the horizon. "That way!" Bernd calls. The two of them fly toward the rising sun. For the first time in ages, Bernd no longer feels lonely. He is capable of flying anywhere he wants. The mountains, woods and lakes are no longer hostile, alien and insuperable obstacles, but exciting and interesting places that he can visit at any time. They have become a part of his new world, and he has a companion in pursuit of the same goal. With her, he can survive any adventure that comes their way. He has an overwhelming sense of connection and security.

Suddenly the fairy shrieks hysterically, "Look out!" Bernd gets such a fright that he forgets to operate his wings, and plummets. It's lucky that he does. A bird with open beak passes right over his head. Bernd sees the fairy is plunging downward, and decides just to let himself fall. But the bird is incredibly agile. With an elegant looping trajectory it turns around and makes straight for Bernd, emitting a battle cry that cuts the air and freezes the blood, and flying like a MiG-29. Free fall would be too slow for escaping the predator. With the strength of desperation, Bernd just manages to execute an evasion maneuver. The bird sweeps past him and seizes the fairy, who is flying a few meters below. "Help! Bernd, help me! Help!" The bird vanishes as it has come. Silently, and taking the fairy with it.

Bernd lands and has to vomit. He is frozen with shock.

"For God's sake, that bird just ate the fairy. These things can't happen, they simply shouldn't be allowed! Fairies surely are privileged magical beings. They can't just get eaten as if they were no better than – well, no better than an ant." Bernd feels first despair, then anxiety, then sadness, and finally a deep emptiness in the heart. "I wish I could hear you telling me what a slow ugly klutz I am. I enjoyed being with you so much, I trusted you so much. And we had made so many plans together! I miss you so much! Where are you?"

Most of all he would like to go back to his anthill, cut off his wings and spend the rest of his days carrying on with his work and grieving quietly. There at least he would be with his own kind. As the proverb says, "Cobbler, stick to your last!" – "Such a silly idea, wanting to find that medicine. If I hadn't done anything, the fairy would still be alive. But can I just go home now? Perhaps she is still alive after all, and desperate for help." Something erupts in Bernd, something that screams and rages, as if a horde of wild Indians were galloping through his head. He breaks out of his lethargy. He will look for the fairy and never rest until he has found her – never mind what it costs. But where can he look? He can't just go asking every bird he meets what it has had for breakfast.

There is no wind, and the midday sun blazes down mercilessly. It is more and more difficult to cope with the heat. Bernd looks up desperately, and thinks, "The light that is touching me right now is touching you at the same moment. If I could only be this light, then we would be together now. How can it be possible that we live on the same planet, under the same sun, in the same environment and breathe the same air and still can't see each other? In the universe, nothing is ever lost. But we always concentrate just on what we haven't got. Why do we always perceive only what keeps us separate?" Bernd decides that from now on he is only going to concentrate on the things that are perceptible both for him and for the fairy. He follows the breath of air, which perhaps has already stroked the fairy. He looks into the light, which perhaps has already bathed the fairy in color, and lets himself be gently led by the impulses that perhaps have already given the fairy comfort and hope.

After a few hours of searching, as he lets himself be led by his intuition, Bernd comes to a stop by a caterpillar. Caterpillars are one of his favorite foods. But this time he isn't hungry. He observes the caterpillar, who is tearing a leaf into small pieces and greedily swallowing them. It doesn't seem to have noticed him.

"Aren't you afraid of me?" Bernd asks. – "I couldn't actually give a hang," says the caterpillar between two mouthfuls. "This morning all my brothers and sisters were eaten by a bird. I'm all on my own. Go ahead and eat me. I'm the last of my kind. What's the use of my becoming a butterfly if I'm going to be the only butterfly in the world?"

"A bird?" Bernd's attention is caught. "Can you describe this bird?" – "Oh, I don't know. It was as fast as lightning, or a MiG-29. Anyway, it was unbelievably fast." – "So?" Bernd asks with excitement. "Where's it gotten to?" – "It must have a nest quite close by," the caterpillar tells him, "but as an ant, you'd better stay out of its way." – "I don't care about being eaten either," says Bernd sadly. "Not because I'm the last of my kind, but because I've lost someone. Somebody who isn't even one of my own kind. Oh and by the way, there are millions or even billions of caterpillars like you in the world. Once you turn into a butterfly with wings, you'll get to meet them." The caterpillar is beside itself with joy. – "For real? You mean I'm not alone?" – "Definitely not," says Bernd, and takes to the air to explore the neighborhood.

Before long a bird shoots like an arrow through the leaves into the sky. Somewhere up there must be its nest, thinks Bernd, and wants to fly upward. But something holds him back and makes him pause. He hears the whispering rustle of the leaves. There's water babbling somewhere. The buzz of a bee falls silent as it lands on a flower. Somewhere a squirrel is nibbling and gnawing at a nut… But wait! Was that a groan?

Bernd goes in the direction of the noise, and sees a twig – no, a small person lying on the ground. "It's the fairy!" Bernd's heart rises into the air like an eagle, as if a heavy weight had fallen off his shoulders. With a single jump he reaches her and takes her in his arms. But she seems practically lifeless, she has no strength at all. Thank God, she is just faintly breathing. "How can I help her, what can I do?" He quickly fetches water, moistens her face carefully and wets her lips.

After a while, the fairy comes to herself. "Please call the medicine man," she whispers. "Find a hollow tree trunk, and drum on it as loud as you can. And say the following verse:

"Infinite universal spirit of life, ground of all being.
In the consciousness of unity with you
we open our hands of light, so that light, love and warmth may radiate
into the hearts of all creatures.

So may the blessing of the All-Highest
flow into the air, the fire, the water, the earth,
all creatures, visible and invisible,
even into the tiniest atom.

So may unity be manifest through the all-embracing
love, wisdom and strength
of the All-One,
and send us Void."

Bernd does as she asks. Where he is standing the air seems to flow into a glass wall. The glass wall suddenly begins to swirl and vibrate. Out of this turbulence Void materializes like an energy that has been there the whole time, but only now becomes compact reality.

Without a word, Void at once goes to the fairy, picks her up, turns round and says to Bernd: "I'll take her with me to save her. You won't see her again. But she will always be there."

Then Void and the fairy vanish.

Bernd is left behind. His heart overflows with happiness at the fairy's being saved, and he feels a deep sense of connection with her. He resolves to go back to his anthill, and share what he has learned with the other ants. Share with them the knowledge that there is no medicine for loneliness, because there is no loneliness. There is only unity.

The Wall

In a distant country lives Victor Von Gnawhausen, a respectable beaver, with his family. It's a family with tradition. For more than a hundred years the Von Gnawhausen clan has been managing the course of the streams in an area of at least three square kilometers, and regulating the water levels. Victor, his wife and their three children are all very proud of the fact. It's their country, these are their streams and lakes, they are the lords of the valley and it's always going to be that way.

But one day a terrible disaster strikes.

It's spring. The winter has been relatively mild, but with a lot of snow. Now the weather changes abruptly. It becomes warm, and pours with rain. A massive snow melt sets in, and the streams turn into raging torrents.

Although normally speaking floods don't present a problem for the sophisticated, elastic dams and dwellings of the beavers, this time it's different. The flood is unusually extreme.

To inspect the remains of the dam and the emergency exits from the beaver house, Victor swims out into the racing waters. He is shocked to find that the water is gradually rising higher than the highest emergency exit. The floods are sluicing mud and branches into the passages and closing off the air supply to the house. Victor starts digging frantically, but the passageway immediately fills up again with mud. The sodden ground has been transformed into a viscous porridge and is sealing off the house, and Victor's family inside it, like a hermetic capsule. He digs and digs desperately for the whole night, till he is totally exhausted. Next morning the water level drops, and at last he can clear the passage. In the house he finds his wife and three children stretched motionless on the ground. The traces of their efforts to escape from the cave can be seen everywhere on the walls. It has been in vain.

What is that now? Did something move? His eldest son gasps feebly. Victor immediately stands over him and shakes him. Breathe! Breathe! Gradually life comes back into his body. Victor's son coughs and doubles up with pain. For a brief moment hope flares up in him – perhaps the others are still alive. But attempts to revive his wife and the two other children are fruitless. Only the eldest has survived.

The next few weeks are a time of pain and mourning. After burying the family, Victor and his son feel paralyzed, powerless, exhausted and cast down. Any planned agenda would be out of the question. And Victor isn't just suffering bereavement. Still more agonizingly painful is the question, "Could I have done anything about it?"

Time passes, and with a heavy heart he sets out to repair the beaver house. With every twig that he inserts, he checks repeatedly to make sure it is laid correctly. This time the structure has to hold. He can't have his only surviving son put at risk again.

Victor works longer and longer, and harder and harder, until he is totally exhausted – every day. The dams get higher and wider all the time. Who knows how bad the next flood will be, how high the water is going to go? All eventualities are taken into account. This time the dam must be perfect. Only the secure feeling that this time the dam will hold soothes the tormenting thoughts which follow Victor every night into his sleep.

Slowly he recovers his optimism. He is proud of his fighting spirit – of what he has achieved. Proud that he hasn't been got down by the hardest blows that fate can throw at a beaver. He is a real Von Gnawhausen.

The sun is uneasily coming over the horizon, when Victor makes a very disturbing discovery: "The lake's water level is rising! How is this possible – in early autumn? The water level never rises at this time of year! Why is fate treating me like this? What have I done to deserve it?" Victor works even more resolutely and persistently on his dams, builds them higher, makes them wider and more solid. This is a battle he has to win.

The day is sunny, warm and beautifully tranquil. Victor sits with his son on a little rise. They enjoy the quiet buzzing of the busy bees and the satisfying, comforting feeling of having worked enough for today. Now they are allowing themselves a break. As they look out over the dams and the valley, something stirs in the thicket behind them. They jump up in fright, and a lady beaver, about Victor's age, emerges beaming from the bushes. "Don't be alarmed, I'm just passing through and I lost my way. Can you help out?"

Victor takes a deep breath. He is ashamed that he, Victor Von Gnawhausen, has reacted in such an uncool manner. He puts on the most indulgent and relaxed expression he can manage in the circumstances, and says, "Certainly I can help you, Madam. Where are you bound for?"

The lady beaver smiles and comes closer. "May I introduce myself? I am Vogola Sinberg." – "Pleased to meet you," Victor responds. "I am Victor von Gnawhausen and this is my son." Vogola smiles at the two of them in very friendly fashion.

"Gee whiz!" Vogola exclaims, and looks out over the valley with wide eyes. "Whatever is that?" Victor stands tall and says with a heart filled with pride, "That is my valley, my country, my home!"

Vogola sits down without speaking and looks flabbergasted. After a while, she bursts out, "You mean to say you built all these gigantic dams? On your own?" – "My son assisted me," Victor says, grinning at his offspring. "Would you like to inspect the structure at close quarters?" – "Yes! This is something I've just got to see!" Vogola exclaims enthusiastically. Victor gives her a lengthy guided tour of the dams and the other waterside edifices. As Vogola trips pleasantly along the dams, the two of them are soon laughing and joking like old friends – just as if they had known each other for ever.

So the afternoon passes into evening. Twilight lies over the land, and Victor offers Vogola a night's lodging. She is pleased to accept. But after just a short time in the beaver house, Vogola becomes uneasy. "Please don't take it amiss," she says. "But I just can't stand it in here. I feel constricted, oppressed and buried. Like in a coffin. I can't breathe properly. I can't explain it, but it's giving me claustrophobia. I'd better sleep outside on the hill, and come back tomorrow morning. Do you mind?" Victor understands Vogola better than she knows. How has he been able to sleep all this time in a room where his family suffocated? How was he able to do that to his son? It's as if scales have fallen from his eyes. He at once resolves to build a new beaver house tomorrow, a few meters further along.

After they have breakfasted together next morning, Victor tells her for the first time what has happened to his family. He's so ashamed, he says, that he hasn't made a new house – that he expected her to sleep in the "family grave", and that only now is he on the point of building a new dwelling.

Vogola listens, much affected, and says nothing for a long time. Then she looks deep into Victor's eyes and asks: "The lake hasn't always been here? But then the lake is an artificial construct! Land sakes, why?"

Victor is completely confused. He expected words of regret and sympathy – and now she's asking him about the lake. Well, of course sympathy and regret aren't going to help much. But how can she just change the subject? Perhaps she is a little bit weird after all. "I don't know either how it's suddenly turned into a lake. And it's getting higher all the time. It's never done that at this time of year before," Victor says.

"Are you kidding me?" Vogola asks. "You dammed up the lake yourself. Your gigantic barrages prevent the water from flowing away. In the Beavers' Manual it is stated that a beaver lake should only have a depth of 60 centimeters. But you've got two meters depth of water. Whatever were you thinking of? It's extremely hazardous and completely unnecessary. That's why I was so frightened in your dwelling. The water, which should actually protect your house, has become a threat to you and your existence. Pull the dams down! Water must be able to flow, otherwise the next flood is going to be an absolute catastrophe."

Victor is beside himself with rage. "What nonsense! Without a protective barrier, everything goes under. I've labored long and hard to create this safety barrier. My personal safety and all my pride are dependent on these imposing structures. And you're asking me to destroy my life's work? Then the whole lake will wash over me and my son and destroy everything. Never! It would be the end of me!" Victor is regretting now having confided so much in this person. She wants to destroy everything that he has created.

Of course you can't just dismiss the danger the dammed up lake represents. But to do away with the dams – that would be just plumb crazy.

Victor asks Vogola to leave. She is casting doubt on his life's work, and that is something he finds insupportable.

In the following weeks, Victor works on a canal to create a more rapid flow of water past his house. This project reduces the water level of the lake to just one meter. That's as far as it goes, however, because the narrow passage between the cliff and the beaver house won't allow a higher rate of throughput.

Fall decks the forest in gorgeous colors. Tints hidden hitherto show themselves, before the big gray of winter, in their full intensity for the last time. Darkness gathers in the skies. Storm winds lash heavy rainclouds over the land. Violent monsoons of rain transform streams into raging rivers. Victor takes his son to the hillock for safety, and inspects the dams with concern. Massive floods are already pouring through the canal. The lake has risen to the top of the dam. While Victor stands in the middle of the dam, the structure collapses. The water plunges down from the damaged point, and enlarges the breach at headlong speed. Victor is just able to cling onto a branch that is firmly anchored in the ground. He clutches it desperately. The floods are trying to carry him away. He feels his strength gradually diminishing.

Suddenly he hears a voice from a great distance: "Let go! Let go! Let go of the branch! If you cling to it for too long, you won't have the strength to swim to the bank! Let the current carry you to safety!" Victor looks in astonishment to the bank, and can just make out a strange beaver, who is waving his arms and gesticulating. Of course he knows he will have to let go sometime. So what is he waiting for? Waiting for someone to tell him what to do? Or waiting till his paws have no strength left, and give up the struggle? Is he afraid he won't make it to the safety of the bank? But beavers are pretty good swimmers. Victor takes heart and lets go. At once the tugging water relents. There are still plenty of whirlpools, but with his excellent swimming skills he makes short work of them. He paddles at high speed along the bank, and finds a fallen tree trunk on which he climbs out of the flood.

Phew! Just made it. But now it's all gone. His dams, his house – everything he has lived and worked for. What did Vogola say? "Pull the dams down. Water must be able to flow."

Why could he not let go?

For the first time in a long, a very long time, Victor weeps again. In him too the flood gates have broken. He cries and sobs, and cannot stop.

After a while, the strange beaver comes along the bank with Victor's son. The child runs to him, radiant with joy, and they have a happy hug. The strange beaver also greets him, evidently relieved. The stranger looks to be out of the ordinary, even dangerous. He is short, with bushy hair, and has war paint on his face – black and white stripes and mysterious symbols on his cheeks and forehead. His cloak is torn, and he holds a knotted stick in his right hand. "I am Elyon, the Wandering Beaver. My homeland is the whole world. Actually I wanted to stop with you for the night. But you seem to be in a bit of a spot. What on earth were you doing on the dam, in this filthy weather? Trying to hold back the water? Well, luckily nothing happened."

Victor looks at Elyon incredulously. "Nothing happened!" shrieks Victor. "I'm finished. I've lost everything. Wife, children, self-respect and now my house as well!"

"That is true and not true," says Elyon, and continues in a sing-song voice:

"I did not register death,
when for the first time
I crossed the threshold of this life.
Oh, what power
opened me into this distance full of secrets,

as a bud opens
in the midnight wood.

When on the first morning I looked up into the light,
I realized suddenly,
that I am not an alien in this world.
The Unfathomable,
which has no form and no name,
took me in its arms – in the arms of my dear mother.

Just so death,
the same Unknown, will meet me as something
that I have known always.
And because I love this life,
I will surely love death in the same way.

The child cries
when the mother takes it away from her right breast,
and finds complete comfort
the very next moment
in her left.

When one day I have to leave,
these be my last words:
Unsurpassable, the things I have seen.
I have tasted the hidden honey of the lotus flower,
which opens on the ocean of life.
And so I am blessed.
These be my last words.
On this stage of limitless forms,
I had my play.

"That is from Rabindranath Tagore," says Elyon, "around 1910. As you can see, truth has not changed." Then Elyon raises his voice: "You do take yourself SO seriously! In your head, the world stands or falls on a beaver dam. That may be so… But now it is time for you to start to take in the truth. Separate yourself from everything! From your wishes, your goals, your past, your future, your emotions, your love, your fear, your rage, your relationships, your child – from everything! What remains? Everything that hasn't been made in your head. Your mental world disappears, and only the truth, reality is left. What you have created in reality you must birth into the Now, every day anew. Only then does it adapt and remain. If you don't, it dissolves. It remains stuck in the past and disappears into a memory. Nothing is intrinsically permanent."

Everything starts spinning in Victor's head. Suddenly vivid pictures and recollections of his earliest childhood come to mind. He sees himself sitting on his mother's lap, and has a clear feeling of deep contentment, perfect connection and total security. A perfect moment, without thoughts or needs. Simply being there, in that moment. Then his mother grabs him and puts him in a play pen. He has the feeling he's done something wrong. He suffers separation. He feels lonely and starts to cry. But he struggles with his tears. He locks himself and his tears into his body.

"Where was I?" Victor comes back to reality. "Oh yes, talking to a wiseacre tramp who's pleased that now I'm as poor as he is. He's trying to convince me that possessions are unimportant, but all the same he wants to stay the night with me. Fine company we keep here!"

Next morning, Victor and his son wake up on the hillock, from which they have a view of the whole valley. Elyon is already awake, and is making tea. The storm has blown over. The sun is pleasantly warm and dries the thoroughly sodden group.

Elyon gives him a friendly smile. In daylight he looks much less warlike, in fact he seems quite harmless. "You'll have to excuse me," he says. "Yesterday I was rather in didactic mode, and it made me inconsiderate." – "Yesterday we were all in an exceptional situation," Victor replies.

After they have drunk an exceptionally delicious tea, they go to inspect the damage. As expected, most of the dam has been washed away. The beaver house has almost entirely disappeared. The canal and a few of the secondary structures are still intact, and it might be possible to repair them. "If you don't mind my staying for a bit, I can help you," Elyon says. "I'm an experienced master builder." Victor has nothing against it. He know all too well how much work is going to be involved. And it's already late fall.

Victor was always proud of the education he had from his father. Friends, relatives and strange beavers have always been inclined to admire his knowledge and his ideas. But what Elyon has to offer puts everything else in the shade. There is nothing he doesn't know, no subject with which he is not acquainted. His imagination and inspiration come from a completely different level. Instead of building massive dams and walls to dam up or push back the water, Elyon makes use of already existing rocks, hills, other landscape features and the subsoil, to influence the current speed and so determine the depth. Bends and whirlpools are created with skillfully devised water engineering and miniature dams. The notable thing is that the current speed is self-regulating, depending on the water volume. From above you can hardly see that the course of the stream has been artificially altered, but the desired effect – protection of the beaver house – has been triumphantly achieved.

Victor slowly comprehends that what he is seeing here is the application of a universally valid principle. Transience and uncertainty are painful to us; consequently we try to wall ourselves in, and keep everything in one place. But the walls, and the holding onto things, are just what leads to the pain we were trying to avoid. We can't hold up changes, we can only let go and flow with the current – then we will find harmony and peace.

Secret Mission

Her fair, almost spotless skin is covered with beads of sweat, which the sunlight makes glitter like jewels. Her forehead and nose are turning red. "All my own fault," Shira thinks. "Why did I let myself in for this nonsense?"

"I know why," says Nubus, her constant companion. "You know very well how important it is for us to hike through these mountains. Your ancestors have always done it, and now it's up to you."

Nubus is a gohm – an etheric being, consisting of energy and spirit. Gohms don't normally show up in the visible world. But this one was saved from extinction by Shira's great-grandfather, almost a hundred years ago. And now Nubus is paying off the debt. He has served Shira's great-grandfather, grandfather, father, and now he is serving the next generation. When Shira came into the world, twenty-five years ago, he chose her as his future mistress. By contrast with her brother, she had a special relationship with her father right from the start, which was very important to Nubus. Now the time has come when his services are to be dedicated to Shira exclusively. For this she must undertake a laborious pilgrimage through the mountains to a spring the gohms hold sacred. Here she will perform a ritual, and then Nubus will belong to her alone. At some time in future she will pass on the gohm to one of her children. If she were to remain childless, Nubus' existence would come to an end. But he doesn't worry too much about that. Shira is extremely attractive, and in health terms as sound as a bell. She is bound to have a family.

"Yes, yes, OK," Shira answers. "How often have I told you that I don't want you reading my thoughts!" – "Why do you say that?" Nubus counters. "I know everything about you anyway. I know you better than you know yourself." Shira gets irritated: "That's what frightens me. You know everything about me, and I don't know anything about you." – "Oh Shira," Nubus says placatingly, "all you need to know about me is that you can trust me and I will always help you. I owe you… But hush, there's somebody coming."

A few meters along the path, an elderly man emerges from behind a boulder. He turns down the path ahead of Shira, and proceeds before her slowly. A minute later she has caught up with. Even from a distance she has noticed the unsteadiness and hesitance of his steps. Now she hears him coughing and wheezing. "Good morning," Shira says politely. "Are you all right?" The stranger stops and looks at her, with tired, rather desperate eyes. "Thank you! If only this backpack were not so heavy… I'm just too old for hikes like this." Shira smiles: "Yes, sometimes less is more," and goes on past him.

"Hey, are you crazy?" Nubus whispers in her ear. "Can't you see what a rough time the guy is having, and you make fun of him? Is this how you were raised?" His reproach affects Shira like an electric shock. She feels she is to blame. How could she have been so heartless? "Okay, I'll sort things out," she thinks, and turns back to the old man.

The latter is still standing where he has halted, and looking at her with expectancy. "You know what," Shira says to him, "since we're clearly going the same way for a bit, I'll carry your backpack until our ways part. In exchange you can carry mine, which I'm sure is lighter than yours." The man looks astonished: "Do you really mean it?" – "If you keep on asking me, I might reconsider," Shira retorts. – "Okay, okay!" the old man says, "I'm happy to accept, even if I find it embarrassing to let my load be carried by such a pretty young lady. On the other hand, I just can't do any more."

"So, are you happy now?" thinks Shira, as she buckles her backpack on the old man. Nubus titters with subdued merriment.

"Good grief, how much does the damn thing weigh?" The very first moment, Shira almost loses her balance. "What on earth have you put in it?" she exclaims, almost hysterically. – "Everything needed for survival," the old man replies. "But I don't actually remember just what it contains. My mother packed it for me." – "What? Your mother?" – "Yes, many years ago. Just before she died, she said, My boy, since I won't be able to look after you in future, I've packed everything you need in this backpack. Take it wherever you go and don't lose it, and you'll always be all right."

The two of them set off, and after just a few steps Shira is deeply regretting her offer. She can hardly remain upright, and wheezes as she adjusts the load on her back. The old man trips lightly ahead of her. "How could I ever have let myself in for such a stupid idea out of guilt? Why didn't you stop me, Nubus?" – "I only told you that you shouldn't make fun of other people," Nubus answers. "The self punishment bit was your own idea. Guilt is only felt when a person thinks he is guilty of something. Now work your guilt off." Shira thinks: "I don't owe the man anything!" – "Not the man," Nubus replies, "but you do owe something to your parents, your education, your conscience and yourself."

After an hour Shira is completely finished. Her knees are trembling. Sweat tickles her skin and trickles down her ankles. Her heart pounds in her ears. Gasping, she asks the old man: "Where are you actually headed for?" – "Oh," he answers, "I'll go wherever you're going. I've never felt so light and unburdened before, while at the same time I've got everything with me that I need."

"Well, that's enough!" groans Shira, and throws the backpack down. "I wanted to help you, not to adopt you! You can go on by yourself. But first let's take a look, and see what you've got in there in the way of indispensable survival aids." – "No, no!" the old man exclaims, "if you open the backpack, something is bound to get lost!" Shira ignores his protest and opens the pack. She can hardly believe all the things that come out of it. A child's gloves, a child's jacket, pants, underwear, and the like, all in child size. In another compartment she finds an ancient loaf of bread, as hard as stone, and a tin can containing some indescribable substance. There are a few old coins, no longer worth anything now, and other trash items. Not a single article is any real use or can be exploited in any way. In addition she discovers a letter written by the man's mother to her son. It gives an idea of the loving care with which she has loaded the backpack. The old man is deeply moved. After so many years, he can mourn for the loss of his mother for the first time, without being crushed by his burden. This letter was the only thing that could have been useful to him in his later life.

The ways part. Shira heads for a pass, while the old man descends into the valley. Nubus is notably silent after this. Rather upset by the business of the backpack, Shira decides to make for a mountain hut for their overnight lodging while it is still afternoon. After two hours of tramping, they find what they are looking for. Apart from the proprietor of the hut and his wife and son, there are just two other guests – two young men who are planning to climb a cliff face in the vicinity.

She is not completely comfortable about the idea of spending the night with strangers in a lonely hut. Nubus is good when it comes to advice, but as an energy being, he can't provide active assistance. On the other hand, surely nothing is going to happen. While the climbers make a cheerful and hilarious impression, laughing and giggling over every triviality, their hosts are silent to the point of gloom. The son serves the food. When she pushes back her plate, Shira notices a scrap of paper. She reads it discreetly under the table: "Please come to the cow byre at 9.00. It's important!"

First she looks at the climbers, wondering if they are responsible – perhaps they want to play a bad joke on her? But their behavior indicates nothing of the kind. The son of the family is equally expressionless.

She goes to bed early. In spite of the exhausting day and her leaden limbs, sleep is not an option. She ponders the message continually. What can be so important, and important to whom? Why all this hugger-mugger? Is it a trap? Nubus seems distracted and clueless. He just keeps murmuring, "I don't like it at all," but he won't say why. After having looked at it from every angle, Shira decides to pursue the invitation. Her curiosity is just too irresistible.

Shortly before 9.00 she creeps through the darkness to the barn. It's a very dark, moonless night. Just a few stars glimmer between the clouds, encouraging you to look out into the universe. Feeling her way, she proceeds carefully to the barn door and opens it. Warm moist air, penetrated by a slightly acidic scent of cowpats, cows and milk, gathers her into a peacefully homely atmosphere. The cows are breathing calmly and evenly. Occasionally a chain rattles. From the far end of the barn, a light approaches. As the light comes closer, she recognizes the son of the family. He gestures soundlessly, inviting her into a stall at the side. Here there is a roughly worked wooden table, where they sit down facing one another.

"Do you know why you two are here?" the boy asks. – "Well, because you told me to come! And what do you mean by 'you two'?" Shira answers. "I am on my own." – "You're lying! Nubus is here too!" Shira is confounded. Nobody apart from her parents and her brother has ever seen Nubus or knows anything about him. He has always been the big family secret. Now this lad is talking about him as if he were a dog on the lead. Worse still, he actually knows his name. – "Who are you? And how do you know Nubus?" she bursts out in a voice loud with tension.

"Your father came this way, your grandfather has been here and so has your great-grandfather. My parents have told me all about your family and Nubus," the boy answers. "Only you, it seems, don't have any idea." – "Come on, let's leave," Nubus whispers. "He wants to manipulate you with some kind of fairy tale. It's dangerous. Who knows what he may have up his sleeve."

Anger rises in Shira. Again somebody who seems to know everything there is to know about her, and she is left looking clueless. "My father told me everything!" she hurls back at the boy. "I don't believe your stories."

"So why didn't he tell you that other people know about Nubus?" the boy asks. She has to admit he has a point.

Nubus is increasingly urgent. "Come on, let's go! There's still time!" But now Shira doesn't want to run away. She wants to know what is going on. – "OK, then why don't you tell me about it," she replies in irritated tones.

"My great-grandfather Wilhelm and your great-grandfather Otto were close friends back in the day," the boy begins. "They were both heavily involved in spiritualism. As far back as 1848 the Americans were crazy about the supernatural, when the Fox sisters had their spirit phenomena. At some point this spiritual fever, so to call it, came across to Germany. There were countless mediums and seers who had contact with spirits or the dead, and foretold the future. In the year 1925 Arthur Conan Doyle, the creator of Sherlock Holmes, actually published a book with spirit photographs.

"At the time, Wilhelm and Otto were taken with the idea of harnessing the spirit world for their own ends. They hired a medium and organized seances at the house of my great-grandfather. Their families took part as well.

"Well, that was how it happened. At one of these sessions, they started by contacting the ancestors. Speaking through the medium, these patiently answered questions and there were some touching moments. But for Otto this was all just a bit nebulous. He wanted to see a spirit at any price. The medium got deeper and deeper into trance, and then Nubus turned up. At the time he was still visible to everyone in the room. The audience were so shocked by the sight that they screamed and wanted to dismiss him at once. But Nubus stayed. That is to say, he became invisible, but he continued to be present. He complained to those present that they had dragged him out of his own world and violated the natural order of things. As a result they had acquired bad luck and immeasurable guilt. In spite of intensive efforts, the medium couldn't get rid of the spirit. He remained in the house of my great-grandfather Wilhelm, and terrorized the family all day long with his comments, rude remarks and threats. From this time on little accidents kept happening. He slowly drove my great-grandparents to distraction. So Otto, who was responsible for the whole problem, decided to look for a person who could get rid of the spirit. From a dealer in African art he learned that there was a shaman in German East Africa who was said to be very successful in exorcising spirits. He was reported to be living near the city of Zanzibar. In his desperation Otto decided to undertake the sea voyage to Zanzibar by way of the Suez canal."

"That's right," Shira interrupts. "Otto gave my grandpa an enthusiastic account of the trip. My grandpa could talk for hours about the fabulous experiences and dangerous adventures of his father."

"Then you must know about the coincidences which led to his encounter with the shaman," the boy continues. "The shaman was terrifying. His body was covered with scars, and it was painted and tattooed all over. He worked with masks, fetishes, dolls, skulls of the dead, probably it was some kind of voodoo. With the help of an interpreter, Otto told him what had happened. Did your grandad tell you what the shaman's answer was?" Shira quotes from memory: "Only when a decision has been taken, can the guilt be overcome. Then the shaman vanished for seven days, going to a sacred place to consult the spirits."

The boy goes on: "And when the shaman came back he brought a small carved wooden statue, a dummy made of plant fiber, bits of animal skin and feathers, a clay bottle with a sacred liquid and a piece of leather on which a map was inscribed. He explained that a certain ritual must be performed to confine the spirit first in the wooden statue, and then the statue must be burned so that the spirit would finally be destroyed."

Shira breaks in excitedly: "Yes, I know about the ritual. It's what I'm supposed to be doing at the spring. But my father never said anything about burning the statue."

"Because it's nonsense!" Nubus shouts in her ear. "If you burn the statue, I won't serve you any longer, I'll make your life hell!"

The lad smiles: "Of course that is what he would say. But believe me, Shira, this spirit is a curse which lies on you and your family. You must destroy him! But to go on with the story. Otto went back to Germany. He was appalled by what he found. My great-grandparents' house was empty. Later investigations discovered that shortly after Otto's departure, the behavior of my great-grandparents changed drastically. Wilhelm and his wife avoided human contact completely, and people kept hearing loud screams, weeping and quarreling coming from their house – quarreling with a third person who evidently wasn't there. The neighbors took note, and they were concerned enough to ring the police. The police found chaos in the house, and my great-grandparents in a completely confused state. After this they were committed to a psychiatric hospital, and their son, my grandfather, was put into care. You can't imagine what they used to do to people in these places. The doctors there saw mental illnesses as diseases of the soul in punishment for sin. So they tried to shake up the soul and bring it to purification by a brutal torture regime. It was the same kind of logic as in the days of witch burning. Sigmund Freud's ideas were quite new back then, and they had hardly penetrated the heads of these doctors. My grandfather still gets tears in his eyes today when he talks about the fearful experiences of his parents. Wilhelm and his wife were broken by these inhuman methods of treatment. And being raised in a care home must have been hell for my grandfather as well.

"Otto blamed himself massively for the whole thing, and was ashamed of his silly idea of wanting to see a spirit. He felt it was a guilt he could never atone for. I guess your grandad was also ashamed of his father. Probably that was the reason why he concealed the real happenings from you and your father. He took the shame and guilt of his father on board and made them his own. Perhaps he also wanted to prevent you and your father from suffering the same guilt that had been a burden to him all his life."

Shira goes quite pale. All at once, some things have become clear. The evasiveness when she asked her grandpa about his past. Now she can sense that she too is carrying something heavy, a feeling of guilt that is almost unconscious and barely perceptible. A feeling that has always been present, which has already become a part of her personality. The hiker comes to mind – the old man who carried his child's backpack around everywhere, as if it were perfectly normal.

Now she feels hatred for Nubus, but at the same time she is still confused. Nubus is supposed to be her friend and servant, isn't he? At least that's what her father always said. "Quick! Go on! What happened next?" Shira asks excitedly.

"Otto searched frantically for the spring where the ritual was supposed to take place. He did have the map, of course, but it wasn't easy to decipher. To begin with he had to find the area that was shown on the map. He spent weeks at the Cartographic Institute, comparing the map of Germany with his less than exact fragment. Finally an area came into focus that showed some agreement with the map. It was the Untersberg in the Northern Calcareous Alps. He set out the same day. He traveled by the same path you have been following. This hut didn't exist at the time. He had to sleep in the open air. My grandfather told me that this was one of the worst nights in Otto's life. Apparently he dreamed he was wandering through country, and got into a bog. He couldn't find a path, and finally found himself getting swallowed up in the morass. Gasping for air and fearing for his life, he started out of sleep and opened his eyes. A beautiful woman was standing before him, dressed in white robes and surrounded in brilliant light. In a clear, soft voice, she said, 'You feel guilty, and have condemned yourself. But there is no such thing as guilt, only responsibility. Take responsibility, and follow your heart. Then everything will turn to the good. Every guilt is paid off, if you live completely in reality.' Then the woman or fairy, or whatever it was, transformed herself into a deer and galloped away. Otto laughed at the time when he told Wilhelm about it, and said, 'A dream within a dream'. But my forebears and I always believed the fairy to be real.

"However that may be, on the following day Otto reached the unknown locality – unknown even to the locals – where the spring was to be found. A beautiful peaceful place hidden in the woods. As soon as he arrived there, he felt fresh and vigorous again. A sip of the water, which tasted good, gave him a feeling of warmth and energy throughout his whole body. Now he was really registering on the senses what it means to talk about a place of power. Following the instructions of the shaman, he gathered stones and laid them in a circle, washed the wooden statue he had brought with him in the water of the spring and placed it in the circle, wetted the dummy with liquid from the bottle the shaman had given him, and then set fire to the whole assembly. Black smoke rose from the burning dummy. Standing in the stone circle, Otto called loudly: 'Nubus, spirit from the world of free energy! Flow into the form that has been allotted to you, flow into the compact substance that has been assigned you! This statue, wetted with the sacred water of your ancestors, is ready to receive you! Appear!' Hardly had Otto spoken the words when Nubus became visible in the smoke. He looked quite pleased, moved toward the statue in a swirl of the smoke and disappeared into it.

"Otto was overjoyed. Finally the spirit had been tamed, and everything was going to be all right. It had been a whole lot easier than he expected. Now all he needed to do was to burn the statue. He fetched sticks from the vicinity and heaped them up over the still faintly glowing dummy. Suddenly he heard a loud yammering of lamentation. It was the voice of Nubus: 'Please don't kill me! You can't just annihilate a living being like that!' Otto responded, 'You've annihilated the life of my friend and his family. You had it coming to you!' – 'I'm really sorry! Just let me make up for it,' Nubus sobs. Otto speaks sharply: 'After the suffering inflicted on them, no one can ever make up for it. It can only be expiated. And that is why you are about to be destroyed!' Otto takes the statue and is on the point of throwing it into the fire, but then Nubus shrieks, 'No, no, I promise by all that is holy that I will never again do harm to anyone. I promise that I will serve you, that I will always protect you and your family. I will even serve your descendants. That can be my way of atoning – just please let me live!' Otto hesitates: 'How do you mean? In what ways can you serve me?' – 'I can see into the hearts of people, I hear what they are thinking. I can tell you what is in their heads, and give you useful hints and advice. I can save you from bad luck, mistakes and deceptions. With my help, you and your descendants can have a successful life.' Otto hesitates. He is still faced with the difficult task, after all, of getting Wilhelm and his family back to normality. He needs to get the parents out of the hospital, and the boy out of the care home. Any kind of support will be worth its weight in gold. Nubus could prove right away that his penitence is real.

"The offer Nubus made was just too attractive to turn down. He decided not to kill him for the time being, put the wooden statue in his pocket and went home.

"Nubus kept his word. He didn't torment my great-grandparents any more. He helped Otto to get Wilhelm and his wife out of the institution, and extract my grandfather from the children's home. Wilhelm sold his house, and they moved away – it didn't matter where, as long as it was a place where no one knew them and they could start afresh. So they ended up here in the mountains. They used the money from the house sale to build this hut, bought animals and lived a self-sufficient life as mountain farmers and hut keepers. It seems it was just coincidence that they built their hut right here on the path to the spring of the gohms. Perhaps the gohms wanted to apologize on Nubus' behalf, by giving my great-grandparents a new home – who knows."

"Wow! What a story!" whispers Shira. "Thank you for telling me all that." It is well after midnight. Shira says goodbye, and stumbles, dead tired, back to her room.

Next morning she appears at the breakfast table very late. The climbers have already left. Shira is feeling even more uncomfortable. When her host serves the coffee, she can hardly bring herself to look him in the eye. She feels small and shabby somehow. Though why? There is no reason at all for her to feel guilty about the past. Besides, everything has turned out fine. Nubus whispers: "He's still carrying resentment. He hates us." Only the boy seems very much more cheerful. Shira packs her things together and says goodbye. She feels she must get out of this hostile environment as quickly as possible, and think it all over quietly. She tells Nubus she doesn't want any clever remarks from him.

The path to the spring turns out to be extremely strenuous. She has to negotiate the steep route to the pass in pitiless heat. On reaching the saddle, she is exhausted. She sits down on a stone and eats a sandwich. Suddenly something moves in the nearby woods. A deer comes out of the bushes and heads directly for Shira. Just a few meters away from her it stops. What does it mean? Nubus whispers, "It wants to tell you something." The deer turns, goes a few steps in the direction of the rock face and looks back at her. Shira understands, and follows the animal. Between boulders, the deer disappears into a cave. When Shira enters the cave, she can hardly believe her eyes. A huge block of ice rises in front of her, which reflects the light falling from above in rich blue and green colors. The whole wall is iridescent, like something out of the Thousand and One Nights. The pleasantly cool air is kind to her overheated body. Pure water drips from the ceiling and makes her skin tingle. Suddenly she hears a voice which seems to come out of the void. Shira goes rigid with terror, her muscles quiver with tension.

Shadows move in the ice and take shape. First they are obscure, then clearer and clearer, till the face of an ancient dwarf emerges. The voice begs: "Please help me. I'm imprisoned here. Please let me out!" Nubus excitedly interposes: "If the dwarf is shut in here, there must be a good reason for it." – "No," the dwarf calls out – "I am innocent! The gohms have banished me here because I killed one of them. But it was self-defense. I felt under threat, and wanted to protect my family. The gohms tracked me down, but I was protected by my people. This was the start of a war between the dwarfs and the gohms. After a long struggle, the gohms won. They took me prisoner and condemned me under gohm law. Under dwarf law, my act would have been seen as self-defense. But the gohms don't recognize that as a mitigating circumstance. As far they are concerned, a deed is a deed, never mind for what reasons or with what intentions the person acts. So everyone must bear the consequences of their deeds. I refused to accept this, and declined responsibility for the killing. I was innocent after all! Now the gohms have imprisoned me in the ice for as long as it takes for me to admit to my crime, and make restitution for the putative injustice. By the universal law of the dwarfs, I will never do that! As a human being, I am sure you understand my position. If your people were to see an action as right and proper and absolve you from any guilt, I am sure you too would decline to accept responsibility."

Shira is confused. On the one hand she thinks just like the dwarf, on the other her heart rebels against this line of thought. She suddenly sees the deer standing by the block of ice, and as if by magic her tangled thoughts become clear. The answer is plain to see. The inner conflict which generally rages in her, above all when she hears talk of wars, melts like ice in the sun. She answers, "Everyone sees justice on their side, every individual has a different understanding of guilt. So the question of guilt is irresoluble. Guilt is an imaginary construct of individuals, made up of their various values, motives, justifications and goals. Without these imaginings, only the deed in itself remains."

The dwarf retorts: "I acted with the agreement of my people when I killed the gohm. I would do it again any time."

Shira continues: "If you know already what you are going to do without being aware of the concrete situation, you are not responding to the circumstances but acting out of conviction. You get caught up in convictions, that is to say in patterns of action and articles of faith which for the most part don't come from yourself but have been fed to you by others. It is quite natural that you refuse to take responsibility for the ideas of others. Persons under orders, imitators and fellow travelers take no responsibility for their actions. But in reality the person who acts is always responsible, whether they like it or not. The act itself gives rise to the responsibility, not the motive or the intent. This is the truth and cannot be changed. With justifications and excuses I can only deceive myself. These are a blindfold with which my perception and my senses remain cut off from the truth. Closing the senses means limiting our perceptions. You create your limits yourself. You create your own prison – impenetrable walls which let no energy out or in, which bring everything to a standstill. The ice around you is the cold which results from your rigidity. Stop trying to deny your responsibility! Throw away the blindfold and open your perceptions. The gohms haven't imprisoned you. You did it to yourself."

Shira leaves the cave. When they emerge, Nubus speaks up: "What was that about? You've never had thoughts like that before, have you?" Shira is surprised herself by her own insights. She thanks the deer and the mountain for her realizations, and ponders the words in her heart.

After two hours of walking, they come to the sacred spring of the gohms. Shira is cheerful and at peace. Everything is somehow coming together in the most natural way possible. Before starting the ritual, she enjoys the quiet of the place as she sits on the edge of the basin.

Nubus interrupts the silence: "Listen, Shira, I've been thinking a lot about what you said in the cave. Is it possible that I too have made myself a prison out of feelings of guilt? That I think like the dwarf?" – "Yes," says Shira. "You think you owe someone your life. As if there could be a right to life which you first have to earn, or which has to be granted, or gifted, by a person who has the power to take it. You think that others have the right to decide whether and how you should live. Long ago when you brought bad luck to Wilhelm and his family, your actions – even if involuntary – then opened up a positive life path for them, and also for Otto. You have transformed your deeds, even if you were unconscious of the fact. This is how someone behaves who assumes responsibility. You can't do more, and you don't need to. Your supposed indebtedness for your life is a self-imposed limitation of your freedom. Your walls go by the names of justice, obligation, guilt, sacrifice and the conviction that what has happened cannot be altered. But all things change and develop continually – even without our doing anything. Nobody has to sacrifice himself for his deeds. We must only exist in love."

Nubus whispers anxiously: "So what are we going to do? Are you going to perform the ritual?" – "Don't worry," says Shira. "Today is a good day to be free. Your eternal idea of guilt must be terminated for all time. It acts like a drug, making your thoughts revolve around it constantly. The drug has determined the life of my ancestors, and your life as well. Do you think I'm going to get addicted? Certainly not! There's nothing left that you need to do for me." Shira takes the wooden statue out of her backpack and throws it in the sacred spring. In the water, Nubus can be reunited with his forebears and the other gohms. He is free.

Shira feels she has let go of something – a burden which has been passed on from generation to generation, an idea which, transmitted unconsciously, has determined her life and the life of her family from way back. A concept containing nothing useful or beneficial, which just limited her freedom of activity. Finally she casts away the backpack with its burden of guilt. Everything she needs for life is already present within her, and the guilt is gone.

School for Dwarfs

In a distant land, deep in the barely populated dark forest, live the Doozlies. Their village is surrounded by fields and meadows painfully wrested from the wide ranging forests, and passed on from generation to generation. The little river near their settlement is their only connection with the outside world and so with their closest neighbors, the Moblies. The remoteness of their habitation has resulted in the development, over time, of a quite distinct linguistic idiom. They use a language in which words are arranged in accordance with thought processes, not in obedience to grammatical rules. The Doozlies and the Moblies carry on lively trade, and get together once a year to celebrate in an uproarious festival. This is an occasion not just for the exchange of goods and news – friendships are forged, and weddings often take place. As a self-sufficient community, the villagers are for the most part farmers or hunters; but trades and other professions are also represented. Each individual is seen as important, and fulfills his or her tasks to the benefit of all.

The following story was told to me by the village wise woman. She is not just a healer, counselor and right hand woman of the mayor; she is also the keeper of traditions and the teller of tales. Her tale was about the village teacher, Abacus.

At the beginning of the story, Abacus was not yet a teacher; he was the eight year old son of the aged master of the village school. It had always been a tradition, with the Doozlies, that sons pursued the same profession as their fathers. So every child knew from an early age what it was going to be, and where and how it was going to live. The strange name Abacus – referring to a calculation device for the teaching of basic arithmetic – had been chosen by the child's father. As a passionate teacher, he saw the calculation aid as a miraculous machine – one that encouraged him to wax lyrical about the Sumerians, Greeks and math generally. For somebody who was going to teach arithmetic to others, he thought the name of a mathematical tool exceptionally meaningful and appropriate.

As the son of the teacher, Abacus enjoyed a special position in the school right from the start. The pupils were afraid of being given bad marks or punished, and assumed that Abacus would tell tales about their derelictions and misdeeds, and as a result he was ostracized and treated with hostility. His father was not just strict with the children generally – he also expected discipline and obedience from his son to an exceptional degree. He was meant to be a model for imitation, just like his father, his grandfather, his great-grandfather and so on had been. He was supposed to tread in their footsteps.

As a result Abacus, at eight years old, was faced with practically insuperable challenges. On the one hand he was an outsider, and nobody wanted to be friends with him; on the other, he wanted to live up to the expectations of his parents, his fellow students and all the other members of the village. He was the future village teacher, after all. But his marks got worse and worse, and the other students harassed him mercilessly. Some of them saw it as a test of courage to play tricks on him in defiance of his father. The lack of appreciation and acknowledgement, hostile and contemptuous treatment, ongoing ostracism and neglect of his needs resulted in his developing an inferiority complex. He thought himself a failure. His father too was ashamed of his son's poor performance. The whole village must be laughing about the fact that he couldn't teach his son anything. Some asked how a person who got such bad marks would ever be able to turn their children into successful students. The teacher's family was desperate. How was Abacus going to live up to his life task and become a good teacher? So every night poor Abacus cried himself to sleep.

One night, after he had again been plagued all day long, Abacus started out of his nightmares to find himself bathed in sweat. It was still pitch dark, and he felt his way – still trembling with the effect of his bad dreams – to the window, to let out the stifling air. When he opened it, cool, moist night air streamed in, smelling of woodland and grass. The meadows and the forest had a silvery shimmer in the moonlight. It was quiet and peaceful. Somewhere in the distance an owl hooted.

Suddenly a twig snapped right under his window. His limbs turned to water as a shadow rushed past. Then a voice whispered out of the darkness: "Abacus! Abacus!" He was barely able to keep his composure and find his voice: "Come out, you coward! I today already sufficiently teased! Enough now it is!" The only explanation, he thought, was that his tormentors were playing another trick on him.

The voice whispered again: "I save you from your fate!" Abacus leaned out of the window as far as he could, and was able to make out a dwarf in the grass. The visitor looked old and wrinkled, but he had a friendly expression, as far as it could be made out in the darkness. "We observe you a long time, you unhappy dumpling. No one likes you. Not even parents love the sad dumpling. They love only their ideas of a dumpling in rich gravy, who one day is going to be head teacher. You don't love sad dumplings yourself either, only ideas of dumplings in gravy." Abacus answered hesitantly: "When I big, I all learned will have. Then me all will like and respect. But now I smarter must become and to fight better learn, for good marks and seriously take myself. You that me teach can?" The dwarf hopped impatiently from foot to foot. "Do I look like a teacher? What for are schools for dwarfs? We have a teacher, she can out of every pupil a good pupil make. We call her Miss Fiery Enlightenment." – Abacus started to laugh, but stopped immediately: "That allow father never. His heart break would, if other school I attend. He think, he not good enough for me." – "Fiddlesticks," said the dwarf. "Hogwash! Come on, I can't hang around all night."

Abacus got dressed, even managing to find some old shoes under the bed, and climbed out the window. The dwarf took him by the hand and they ran toward the forest. There they made for a boulder. Though Abacus knew every inch of the forest, he had never seen this boulder before. The dwarf pushed a bush to the side, and the entrance to a small cave came into view. Abacus had to crawl in on all fours, but soon the passage became more spacious – or had he himself shrunk? Perhaps the dwarf had grown? At all events they were now the same height.

"Come on, we'll go by Taxi-badger," said the dwarf. Abacus had only ever seen horse drawn carriages, so he was incredulous when two badgers emerged out of the darkness. Badgers are powerful animals, well capable of carrying a very small human being or a dwarf. Glow worms sat on their heads and illuminated the passage like headlamps. The rather grumpy badgers just looked at the pair inquiringly, after they had mounted. The dwarf called out,

"To the School for Dwarfs!" – and the adventure began. They passed through endless dark passageways, with stalactites, waterfalls, streams and deep ravines. Sometimes they traversed gigantic halls where precious stones glittered in the walls, or gold veins broad as an ell emerged from crevices. At some points sunlight penetrated the darkness, falling from the cave ceiling in bright columns. These places seemed like oases from another world, being overgrown with ferns and strange vegetation. It was some time before the badgers suddenly halted in front of an inconspicuous iron gate. When the pair got off their backs, the badgers disappeared as swiftly as they had come.

The dwarf applied pressure to two rusty nails in the middle of the gate, and murmured in an undertone, "Open sesame!" A disquieting subdued rumble followed, and the earth shook slightly. The gate slowly started to move, and a powerful draft blew through Abacus' hair. He and the dwarf squeezed through the narrow opening, and the gate closed after them.

Beyond the gate it is friendly, bright and warm. A massive hall opens. At a few points sunlight streams in, reflected into all corners by silver mirrors. Abacus can't get over his astonishment. It's a complete dwarf city. There are little houses built on different steps and levels. Some are suspended from the walls. All the houses are linked by a tangle of paths, stairs, ladders, stone walkways and wooden suspension bridges. A stream runs through the middle of the city. It's a bizarre, cute, merry little world. They pause until Abacus recovers from his astonishment and is again capable of speech. Then they proceed till they come to a fairly big building. Over the entrance is written, in large letters, SCHOOL FOR DWARFS.

Abacus is unpleasantly affected. Just the very thought of entering a school gives him a sense of inhibition and guilt. But they enter, and he is shown to a bench outside the classroom. The dwarf goes to announce their arrival to the teacher. He feels it has been an age, when the dwarf comes back with a small and strange looking lady dwarf. "This is the teacher's son," the dwarf announces proudly. The teacher, who has a face like a toad's, puts on a broad smile and says, "Hello, Abacus! I've been expecting you for a long time! Finally we meet!" Abacus is surprised. "How come you me know?" – "Oh, I'll tell you that later. Come with me into the classroom. The lesson must go on. Oh by the way, I am called Ruby."

In the classroom, fifteen pupils are sat in a circle. It is so quiet you could hear a pin drop, and they are all staring fixedly at a rose in the center of the circle. Abacus joins them, and looks with confusion at the faces of the others, and at the rose. Then Ruby takes the rose away and calls, "Go!" On this command, they all jump up, yell, chatter and sing confusedly, and rampage chaotically around the room. Finally the children sit down in small groups at tables, and start to draw with the crayons and paper provided. Abacus is a bit lost, and looks at Ruby. She smiles: "Sit down somewhere and paint the rose from memory. Don't just paint any old rose, but exactly the rose you have seen."

Abacus grabs paper and crayons, and is about to start. But then familiar feelings – of anxiety, helplessness, grief – surface in him again. What is he supposed to draw? Not just any old rose, but exactly the one I have seen? If only I could remember what the rose looked like. What makes this rose different from other roses? How can I possibly bring it off? I can't draw well, or accurately. Tears fill his eyes, and he doesn't dare to make a single mark on the paper, for fear it may be wrong. Meanwhile the other children are laughing and drawing merrily away. Eventually Ruby comes around to his table: "Abacus, what's the matter? You're not drawing anything." – "It sorry me makes, Mrs. Teacher," Abacus replies tearfully, "but I not able do that. I not notice how exactly rose look, and if I knew, not draw can so like you wish."

The other children look at him in surprise. One of them says, "How so? You should only draw what you have seen, not what you have not seen." Ruby gives Abacus a hug, and goes on: "Draw the rose as you see it, not as the others could have seen it or I could have seen it, because you can't know that. That is not possible. Don't try to fulfill the supposed expectations of others, because it doesn't work. Do what is right for you, as the others do what is right for them. If your actions don't meet their expectations, that's their problem. But I'll explain that later. Come with me, let's look at the roses the other children have drawn."

And indeed, the other children have drawn roses that look quite different from the one he has seen. Some have seen a yellow rose, some a blue one; there are little buds and there are massive blossoms. Each of them has clearly seen something different, something very individual. Abacus looks Ruby in the eye: "And who best and who worst mark get?" – "Well," Ruby replies, "as each has drawn exactly what they saw, I have to award them all top marks. How could I prove that someone has not drawn what they have seen?" That does make sense somehow.

In the break, the dwarf children flock around Abacus, asking him where he comes from and what it's like there. To them his tale is a real horror story, and some start to cry. How can he have survived in this land of zombies? With a life totally determined by parents and the other villagers? A life where it is all laid down who you are, what you are going to be when you are grown and how much respect you deserve? This is a recipe for sorrow and pain. Some children share their snacks with him, wanting to show their sympathy and support.

Then it's the start of the next lesson. A cuckoo calls, three times exactly, and the children run excitedly into the classroom. Ruby is always coming up with surprises. "Today we are going on an outing." – "Yippee!" the children cry, and quickly gather their things together. Meanwhile one of the children asks where they are going. "Abacus can decide today, since he's new here," Ruby answers. Abacus goes hot and cold: "But, I not know here!" Ruby replies with a laugh, "That's what makes it special. You explore the unknown dwarf country, and we go with you on your voyage of discovery. That makes it as if we were discovering a new country as well!" A dwarf girl calls, "I want to go to the waterfall!" – "I want to go to the magic cave," another girl cries. – "No," yells a boy, "I want to go to the squirrels and ride!" Each of the pupils comes up with a different suggestion, all suggesting places that in their view are the most beautiful and unmissable. Abacus is quite dizzy with all these alternatives. "We only one of these can see and I not know where we go," he says. Immediately other children offer to be the leader, but they can't come to agreement on a common destination. Each one insists on his or her favorite spot. Abacus turns to Ruby for help. She says, "Today is your day. You decide where we go. Nobody is allowed to guide or advise you. You alone decide."

Abacus feels sure that whatever he decides, he is going to make himself unpopular with the majority. How can he get out of this situation in such a way that they will all still continue to like him?

First he apologizes to the children for the fact that he can't meet their wishes. Instead of being pleased with his apology, they all become sad and despondent. Each of them has the feeling they are not being given something which they actually had a right to.

Ruby interposes: "Nobody should apologize for decisions. Apologies only make sense, if at all, when you have unintentionally damaged somebody and are unable to restore the damage. But this is a very rare occurrence. Mostly the assumption of guilt for the unfulfilled wishes of others is just arrogance. You are suggesting to the other person in this way that you are responsible for their wellbeing and their wishes, which of course is not true. Each person is responsible only for his or her own life, and that of those they are obliged to care for. So apologies are an attempt to place yourself above the other person or take possession of them. Your fellow students are now unconsciously assuming that you are responsible for their being, and they have surrendered their responsibility to you. The result is that they now feel helpless, because you can't fulfill their wishes. So don't apologize, but say what you want to explore! They are all supposed to imagine that they are discovering this terra incognita, the unknown land, along with you."

The children look to Abacus expectantly, and he calls out: "That way!", extending his arm to the south. The children cheer, spontaneously line up behind him and the troop gets moving. They go over bridges and paths, up hill and down dale, passing pretty houses and well tended gardens. Soon they leave the city behind them, and are marching on paths that get narrower and narrower. The trail twists between trees and rocks, and the children fall silent. One child says, "Soon we'll be coming to dragon country." They have left the trail some time back, and now reach a small pond. On the other side there is a very ancient hut with a smoking chimney. It is so overgrown with ivy that only a window and a door are still visible. In the middle of the pond something floats, looking like a ball or a globe. It has a golden gleam, and moves up and down as if the waves were rocking it. Only there aren't any waves to be seen.

"What's that?" the children ask. Ruby says, "That's for Abacus to explain. It's his trip, he has brought us here."

First Abacus is on the point of apologizing, but then thinks better of it. "I also not know what this is, but want find knowledge." Cautiously they go along the bank toward the hut. As they approach, they hear voices coming from the hut: "Wrong! It's all wrong! Who is responsible for this garbage? Can't you do anything right? How does this look? I'm going crazy! You miserable failure!"

"The poor guy, what can he have done?" Abacus wonders, and he knocks on the door. "What is it now? Who's bothering me this time?" shrieks the voice from the hut. "Er, apology I disturb here!" calls Abacus, while considering whether the word "apology" is really appropriate. He hasn't done any harm after all. So in this case it is probably just a meaningless politeness. "I want ask you!" – "Ask? Ask?" the voices reply. "Everyone is always wanting to ask things. What am I, an information bureau?" The door opens, the grumbling and scolding continuing all the time.

Abacus finds himself facing a being – no, three beings who have grown into one. The creature looks like a child on whose shoulders two extra heads have grown – the heads of an old man and an old woman. And they look so ugly. On their long necks they move excitedly back and forth, muttering ugly things to themselves. Everything the child does, every movement and every thought, is commented on, condemned, rated and dismissed. "Why ever did you open the door, you stupid child," the heads hiss. "It could have been a serial killer or the big bad wolf. You need looking after the whole time, otherwise you just do stupid things." The child gives Abacus an embarrassed smile. "Hello, I'm Fanti – actually Introfantia, but that sounds so formal. Who are you?" – "Oh, er, I Abacus am," he answers, still completely bewildered by the strange phenomenon. "Something like you never yet seen have I!" – "Yes, I haven't always been like this, but that is a long story," says Fanti, and now notices the other children and the teacher. "Hello Ruby!" she calls, beaming. "Long time no see!" One of the heads adds: "I knew it was going to be a terrible day." The other agrees with a vigorous nod. Ruby gives Fanti an affectionate hug and asks, "Are you lot finally getting on OK?" – "It'll be a while," Fanti answers. The heads look awkwardly at one another, and sputter: "Why are we punished with this child? It's all your fault," says the male to the female head. The other shrieks back, "I only did you a favor! And that's how you thank me! Besides, she takes after you! You've always had bees in your bonnet!" The male head turns to Ruby: "We would come to an agreement, you know, but the child is so useless. We're always having to help it and tell it off. How can you hope for any kind of agreement, given the situation?"

Ruby looks at Fanti: "You're giving them too much power. How about if you tell us how it all happened?" Fanti invites the dwarf children into the hut, promising them a story. The room, which functions as a sitting room, kitchen, dining room and bedroom in one, is actually too small for their number. So they put the table and chairs out the door. Then they all sit on the floor, and each is given a glass of water. Fanti sits on the sideboard so that everyone can see her, and starts her tale:

"Once upon a time I was an elf, and lived with my parents in this elf tower. Back then all the rooms were still intact, and there were beautiful flowers everywhere. I used to play all day, or go swimming in the pond. One day I came home, tired from playing, and found my parents gone. I called to them, but there was no response. The earth seemed to have swallowed them up. It was beginning to get dark, and I got more and more anxious. It was past dinner time and still they didn't show up. Nobody fixed a meal for me. Now I'm going to starve, I thought, and started crying. Where, oh where are my parents? Then a strange elf in black robes came by. She looked me earnestly in the eyes, and said, 'Why are you crying, my child?' – 'My parents have disappeared, and without them I'm going to die!' I told her. The black elf said sadly, 'Yes, my child, you may well be right there. Your parents always tell you what you must do. They know best about everything. Without them, you are lost.'

"How right she was! Without parents, I was lost. I begged the elf: 'Please, please help me!' – 'Well,' she said, 'just imagine your parents are not gone but are still here. You know the things they like to say, you know just what they think of this and that and what they would advise you or tell you to do. If you can imagine all this really vividly, it's just as if they are still here. Your fears will disappear, and you will feel safe again.'

"'It doesn't work! I can't do it!' I complained. 'My sadness is a whole lot stronger than my imagination. It will melt my imaginings like ice in the sun.' The elf considered, then she said: 'I'll give you something that will help you. From now on, there will be a golden ball in the middle of the pond. Whenever you feel weak, sad or lonely, look at the ball. Then you will feel your power.'

"And indeed, since that time a golden ball has been floating in the middle of the pond. Whenever I am sad, I look at it – then I have sweet dreams, and feel quite at home.

"My parents have never come back, and I have become a real expert in imagining them. In the course of time, their heads actually grew on my shoulders as a result of my vivid imagining. Oddly enough, though, these heads are just exaggerated caricatures. In reality my parents were never so ugly or so dismissive. These heads treat me as if I were three years old and didn't have any personality of my own. They belittle me and make me nervous with their constant criticisms, and I would really like to be rid of them. On the other hand, without them I would be dreadfully lonely."

Ruby observes that this is a good example of the way in which some things, which are originally good and beneficial, at some point become damaging and inhibiting. When we don't constantly examine things or adapt them to the actual situation, they easily turn into a caricature or become their own opposite. This can also happen when we try to keep everything the way it was in the past. Not wanting to change things only means that we turn a blind eye to them. As a result we don't notice the changes to begin with, but at some point it becomes impossible to ignore them.

"Abacus," Ruby says, "what do you think Fanti should do?" Abacus considers. Actually, he's got scolding critical parents in his own head. But without their criticism, he isn't sure what is right or wrong either. Without their advice and their judgments, he feels lost.

He answers: "I say, Fanti something other needs, which better helps, which even without parents helps." The heads start to scold and rage, till Ruby sternly tells them: "Silence!" They fall quiet instantly. "Abacus is right! Fanti has something much better than these annoying parental substitutes. She only needs to bring it into the house." Everybody looks at Ruby expectantly. What can she be on about?

Fanti's eyes are shining: "The ball, the golden ball!" – "Yes," says Ruby. "When you've gotten that, you don't need parents any more."

But it isn't all that simple. The ball is in the middle of the lake, and Fanti is afraid to swim across the lake on her own. Abacus, who is a good swimmer, says he is prepared to go with her. The water is icy. It takes a great effort to immerse oneself completely. Trembling and with goose bumps, they swim toward the ball – Abacus in front, Fanti close behind him. Fortunately Fanti is so preoccupied with the freezing temperature that she can't pay any attention to her worries, or to the furious comments of the heads. It's strange – as they approach the ball, the water gets warmer. Finally Fanti can reach the ball, where it bobs up and down. Oops! It seems to be much heavier than she expected. She tugs at the ball but can't move it from the spot. It's as if it were somehow anchored. Suddenly air bubbles start coming up out of the depths. The water starts foaming and swirling. Abacus and Fanti paddle like crazy so as not go under. Something seems to emerge from the depths, while the ball sinks in the water.

Quite slowly, the head of a small dragon appears on the surface of the water. Abacus holds his breath. Its mouth is enormous and arrayed with sharp teeth. "It's curtains for us," he thinks. But the dragon doesn't gobble them up. On the contrary he seems well disposed, even looks at them in a friendly way and addresses them gently: "At last! It was about time. Do you actually know how long I've been waiting for you, Fanti?" Fanti, whose face is still deathly pale, stammers: "What? How come? Er, how come you've been waiting?" – "The ball was just a buoy, to show you where to find me!" the dragon replies. "You've been looking at it every day and never thought to ask what it was. Well, at all events, you have found me now. I am your very personal protector and companion dragon. From now on, you don't need those awful heads any more." With two blasts of fire the dragon burns the vocally protesting heads off Fanti's shoulders, and it is as if two heavy weights have been removed. She feels liberated and happy. Radiant with joy, the three of them swim to the bank. The children and Ruby have followed the spectacle and so know there is no cause for alarm, because it is a lucky dragon.

By this time it is late afternoon, and the children have to go home to their families. After they have all said goodbye to Fanti and her dragon, they go back to the dwarf city. This was the most exciting outing they have ever experienced. Abacus too needs to go back to his parents. The Taxi-badger is waiting already, and takes him back to the cave mouth in the wood. In three days' time, the badger will fetch Abacus to the dwarf school for another lesson.

Getting back to his room, he just has time for a short nap before getting up to go to his own school. He is dead tired, but all the same feels relaxed and in a good mood. He doesn't care what his parents, the other pupils or anyone else expect of him, from now on he just does things as he sees fit and in whatever way he thinks best. He no longer needs any judgments or words of advice from his parents or from anybody. In the following days, his behavior changes radically, and so does that of the other students. His clear and confident decisions and opinions make him more respected and looked up to every day. His school performance improves as well, along with his concentration.

On the night of the third day, he waits with eager anticipation for the Taxi-badgers who are to take him to the school for dwarfs.

Ruby and the other dwarf children greet him joyfully. "Guess what we're doing today," a boy bursts out. "We're invited to a birthday party!" – "Yes," laughs Ruby. "Mr. Orbo has invited all the children to his hundredth birthday. It will be a fabulous party. Think what you are going to take Mr. Orbo as a present. He's very rich and lacks nothing, but presents make him happy as a sandboy."

Most of the children fetch the rose pictures they drew the other day. Some have sweets which they wrap up nicely in colored paper tied with a ribbon. Only Abacus can't think of anything. His rose picture is in his room back home, and he hasn't got anything else with him. If only he had known. Mr. Orbo will surely be very disappointed.

Mr. Orbo's estate is enormous, and surrounded by high walls. After having been admitted by a gatekeeper, they cross the extensive park. They pass moats, pavilions and farm buildings until a chateau comes into view behind the trees. It has little turrets, bay windows and numerous side wings. A fabulous building, more suitable for a king than for a centenarian grandad. Marquees and tables are set up in front of the chateau. Half the dwarf city is already assembled. As they approach, Ruby explains that Mr. Orbo is the richest dwarf in the country. He lives as a recluse, and very few have ever seen him. Nonetheless he knows about everything that happens in dwarf country, and quite frequently intervenes through his emissaries to affect the course of events.

In front of the castle, one of the servants is taking delivery of the presents, carefully writing the names of the givers down. When it comes to Abacus' turn, he wilts with embarrassment. The servant writes down, "Abacus has brought nothing." In desperation Abacus blurts out, "I Mr. Orbo story from my life tell can!" The servant erases the record, and instead writes down, "Abacus gives a story from his life."

The schoolchildren and other guests are treated to a sumptuous banquet. Acrobats and clowns provide entertainment, and some dwarfs recite poems, sing or perform theatrical sketches. It's a relaxed, convivial and entertaining occasion. Only Mr. Orbo is nowhere to be seen. The servants explain that it is unfortunately impossible for Mr. Orbo, in view of his advanced age, to attend the party. But he is observing everything carefully from a window, and he can also hear the recitations and the singing. He would like to thank everyone for their presents and express his appreciation that so many people have come to his party.

Late in the afternoon, one of the servants whispers in Abacus' ear: "Come with me into the house, Mr. Orbo wants to see you." Oh God, Abacus thinks, now Mr. Orbo is going to complain about his non-existent present. He looks out for Ruby but can't see her. As the servant insists, he will have to go alone.

Inside it is even grander than the building looks from the outside. The halls and rooms are decorated with beautiful stucco. Colored pillars and marble floors alternate with modern glass structures and rustic woodwork. Finally the servant stops in front of a richly decorated, gilded gate. He opens a wing of the door and shows Abacus in.

Abacus finds himself in an impressive library. In the center of the room there is an armchair or throne on a podium. Dwarfs stand around the throne with their faces turned toward Abacus, forming a circle. These dwarfs look strong, and with their wild and resolute faces, even quite dangerous. Abacus can just sketchily make out a small shape which almost disappears on the massive throne. "I welcome you, Abacus," says a thin reedy voice. "I am Orbo, the richest dwarf in dwarf country. Come closer so I can see you." Hesitantly Abacus approaches the bodyguards, who immediately close ranks. Only now can he clearly see the old, sad looking dwarf in gold embroidered garments. Next to the dwarf there sits a little monkey, who excitedly climbs up the throne and down again, tugs at Orbo or jumps on his head. Orbo is clearly having a hard time keeping the money under control.

"I'm sorry about the guards," Orbo says. "When you're as rich as I am, you have lots of enemies and enviers. I was told that you've brought me a story from your life. Although I've heard a lot about the Doozlies, a first hand story would interest me much more than any travel reports. I'm already looking forward to it immensely." At the last words, the monkey pulls his nose so forcibly that Orbo emits a cry.

"The monkey I should remove?" Abacus asks. "Then can hear story without distraction." Orbo laughs: "That would be very nice, but unfortunately it's not possible." Abacus is confused: "How come?" In sad tones Orbo says: "You can't enter the circle, and I can't get out of it. Nobody gets past the guards." – "How then the monkey gets to you?" Abacus asks. Orbo groans: "In former times there were fewer guards, and I could make contact with my environment without a problem. At that time, this adorable monkey visited me, and we had fun playing together. At some point the guards' ring of steel suddenly became so tight that the monkey couldn't get out any more. Now we are both locked in." Orbo whistles through his teeth, as the monkey bites his toes. "The animal has turned into a pest now, and makes my life a living hell."

"Guards remove and monkey go can!" Abacus exclaims. – "Are you crazy?" Orbo retorts. "Who's going to protect me then? It would be much too dangerous!"

Abacus considers briefly, and then launches into his story.

"When it happened, very small I was. Always remember that, mother said. It was like this: we good neighbors had, lots of conversations. I was baby, they also baby had, only two weeks older was than me. Came from the neighboring village a Moblie one day. Strangers he was looking for, who stolen had child from him. He want to know if we seen or heard of strangers. No one knew anything, no one help could. But news of dangerous strangers like forest fire spread in village. Our neighbor very frightened he was his child stolen might be, so he closed windows, doors, everything tight as tight. Even when he at home, he close everything. A fortress his house become. But after pass some time, fire rages in his house. Everything in flames was and burning brightly. Fire department to save him try, but not in can come, because tight closed everything. Inside neighbor can't come out, because tight closed and smoke too thick to open. All burn up except for baby. Baby cries in garden under bush and is found. Miracle. Nobody ever know how it happened and who saved baby. Who out of closed house can baby fetch? After that village elders new parents find for the child.

"Mother say, from this you learn can: walls and barriers on both sides walls. Danger from outside can't come in, danger from within can't get out. We blind for danger within, we look only to outside. So wall not remove danger, but only separate different dangers from one another. Safety is illusion. Danger is always there. But when no wall our vision distorts, we all dangers see and defend us can. Vulnerability we see and accept can. Then we strong are and can win."

Mr. Orbo is suddenly very still. Tears run down his cheeks. Then he says: "Now I am a hundred years old, and I am still afraid that someone is going to kill me. And I had quite forgotten that my death will be my own dissolution. The guards are looking to find danger in the wrong direction. Go away, you guards! I don't need you."

The guards look at one another in confusion. Then Orbo calls again in commanding tones: "Go!" The guards march reluctantly out of the room, and the space somehow seems to have become lighter. Mr. Orbo sits peaceably smiling on his throne, with the monkey sitting quietly beside him. The monkey is so stunned, it doesn't know how to behave. Then Mr. Orbo says: "Abacus, you've given me the finest present I've ever had. You have given me freedom. I will find a way to show my gratitude to you. Thank you so much!" Then the throne and the podium sink into the floor and disappear, and Abacus is left alone. He goes back to the others.

When it gets dark, Ruby gets all the children together and they leave the party. The children go home, and Abacus is taken to the badgers. When Ruby says goodbye to Abacus, she hands him a package with a twinkle. "Mr. Orbo told me to give you this from him. But only open it when you get home."

Abacus can hardly wait to be in his own room again. In the package he finds a golden ball and a piece of paper. The paper reads: "The ball is a dragon buoy. When you rub it, your personal lucky dragon will appear and protect you from all dangers. Live how you see fit, because your own vision is all you can know. What is true for you, is true. Know that there is only freedom! Live freedom without fear. Only fear makes us think that there are constraints. However your life will be, whatever path you may tread, the dragon energy is always with you."

The little god

Once upon a time there was a little god, who just couldn't get enough of playing with the angels in the golden sunlight. The great God was delighted to see this, and he called the little god into his presence.

"I've got a present for you,' he said.

The little god squeaked with delight and excitement. He loved presents more than anything. Presents from the great God, in particular, are always something special.

Now you need to be told, gods don't wrap their presents in wrapping paper with a ribbon. That would spoil the surprise, because little gods would have no difficulty peeping inside the paper. Gods hide their presents in the remote distances of the universe. When you have billions of suns and a whole lot more planets, a small god fails to keep count and isn't going to notice if something has been added that isn't actually supposed to be there.

The two of them travel on a light beam through the boundless distances of the universe. The little god calls, "Faster! Faster!" He simply can't wait. Finally they stop in front of a beautiful blue planet which sparkles in the light of its sun.

The little god claps his hands with joy. "Oh! It's really beautiful! Is that for me?" – "Yes," says the great God. "I must say it's turned out rather well. I call it earth, and it's for you, for your very own." The little god laughs happily and embraces him: "Thank you so much! That's the most beautiful thing I've ever been given. I must take a closer look at it right away."

Only now does he discover the real beauty of the gift. Somewhere on the planet, a sunrise in gorgeous colors can be seen at any time. On the opposite side, an even more colorful sunset will be taking place. There is always day and simultaneously night on the other side, summer at the top and winter down below and vice versa. All kinds of weather can be found on the surface of the planet simultaneously: sunshine, rain, storm, tropical heat and so on. In some regions even weather combinations can occur – for example, snow and warm sunshine together, or rain and hail in tropical heat. Clouds form swirls with many arms, cluster into tower-like formations or artful abstract paintings. The whole planet is a sea of colors, forms, scents and flowing materials. The surface is populated by brightly colored plants and animals which with their behavior and their organization constitute a perfect interlinked system.

A fantastically interesting, richly varied world in 3-D with surround sound, backed up by authentic touch and scent and in super resolution. Wow!!! The great God has really pulled out all the stops.

The little god can't get over his amazement, and spends many centuries investigating and observing the world. But the best thing about this present is that he can intervene in this world and make changes happen, without having to press buttons or operate a keyboard. He can take on an animal body, and so influence happenings – and it also enables him to feel and perceive what is going on. It's such fun, being in a body like this.

He particularly likes the bodies of a quite particular species. He calls them humans. Their feeling range, their cleverness and their pleasing physical structure are just fantastic. Only their intelligence still needs a bit of tinkering, so as to make it less of an effort converting intentions into actions. Another advantage of these humans is their favoring close social links, and their excellent team spirit. By contrast with other herd animals, they don't just interact within their own family or clan – they can also cooperate and communicate with complete strangers. This boosts the possibility of making large scale changes happen to an enormous degree.

In order to test the limits of their cooperativeness and performance, he gets zillions of people building a massive pyramid with the most primitive tools.

Centuries pass. With the help of human bodies, the little god is really enjoying this world to the full. He can do everything, have everything, experience anything he wants. Nothing is dangerous for him. Well, of course humans have fragile bodies. They easily become sick, break down easily, and even when well looked after, they have a limited shelf life. But the god is present in all human beings simultaneously… and new births constantly swell the numbers. So the death of one body is sad, but acceptable. By this time there are human beings in their millions.

After many hundreds of years, the little god has tried everything, experienced everything and plumbed the depths of every feeling. He's starting to get bored.

So he decides to give the game a quite special incentive. By changing the rules, in such a way that even a little god will be taken to his limits. The very idea of it gives him a feeling he has never known before: apprehension. "This is going to be fascinating," he thinks. "I want to know what it's like not being a god. I want to forget that I am divine, that I can do anything, influence or have anything I want. I want to know what it's like to be vulnerable and mortal."

But how can you forget? How can you just forget who you are?

To begin with he tries to imagine that everything that happens is quite independent of him and his will. That everything is somehow controlled or dictated from outside… He tries to convince himself that everything happening to him is caused by other humans, by chance or by fate. Sometimes he actually pins the blame on the great God… He himself is just a victim of circumstances, without any power or influence on events.

But in the long run it doesn't work. Things keep happening which remind him of the truth of his divinity. This victim thinking just doesn't seem to come off.

So he resorts to a trick. He must divert his attention from the truth to such an extent that it can just be overlooked. Then he will be able to believe his own lies. His spirit must continually produce ideas and problems which will preoccupy him in such a way that clear thinking becomes impossible. The ideas must revolve relentlessly around themselves, assess everything, judge everything and convert it into a problem.

No sooner said than done. All at once he thinks (and with him all human beings who are inspired by him) only about problems and solutions, mostly those associated with emotionally based value judgments... Human beings, and the little god, now feel that they are helplessly at the mercy of fate. They are afraid – afraid of the future, of sickness and death. They no longer perceive their creative abilities and opportunities.

The little god and humanity with him forget their divinity.

This goes so far that they actually start shooting themselves in the foot without being aware of it. It happens more and more frequently that the little god wants to fulfill a wish, but secretly thinks, "That's never going to work," or "I'll never be able to do that." And as he is an almighty god, naturally everything that he really believes becomes reality... So just as he wishes, it doesn't work.

Even worse is that he no longer perceives his simultaneous presence in all bodies. He can only sense the one body on which his consciousness happens to be currently focused. As a result he feels incomplete, lonely, vulnerable and mortal. The ability to bring about big changes by joint effort – like in the building of the pyramids – is gone. Large scale projects only succeed now by means of a barter system, in which every person has an eye only to his own advantage.

For many centuries, he – and with him, human beings – stagnate in this state, sinking into a morass of anxiety and neediness.

The great God was pleased initially by the enthusiasm that the little god showed for his present. But now that a long time has passed, and nothing has been seen or heard of him in all this time, he finally decides to check it out.

The blue planet is not sparkling so brightly as it was to begin with. Some animal species have become extinct, and the ecosystem is pretty much broken down.

He calls the little god – and there's no answer.

Now he really needs to talk to him! The little god, who now inhabits billions of human beings, reacts in a most unusual way. He asks: "Who are you? What do you want of me? Please don't hurt me!"

To begin with the great God is surprised by this strange and senseless reaction… But then he understands, and laughs loudly for a long time. "Evidently you've been playing much too long! Your perception has become so foggy that you can't see the truth any longer. You have forgotten who you are! Perhaps you are still too small for a planet of your own. Come with me, let's go back to playing with the light and the angels."

"But if I leave now," says the little god, "then all these human beings will be no better than intelligent animals. Without my inspiration, without my suggestions and my higher consciousness, they will never be able to manage. Can I just abandon them?" – "You are right!" says the great God. "You caused them to disrupt the original balance when you breathed intelligence into them, and now you should take responsibility for your actions."

The little god thinks for a long time, trying to find a solution. Then he resolves to leave every human being his own divinity. Each human being, even without him, should be able to determine and influence what happens to them and their environment and should have their own godlike inspirations.

In future, they too will be a gods at play.

The Zardos

The meeting

In a distant country, sixteen year old Peter lives with his family. His parents are not particularly rich, but not particularly poor either. In our terms they would be seen as a middle class family.

Peter's friends are Andreas, Andreas' little brother Pauli, Robert and beautiful Anya. The friends are very different. Andreas is a logical, clear thinking person, a very good chess player; Robert is sporting, strong and a brave warrior; Anya is responsible for romanticism and emotions. She is a cheerful girl without problems, and everyone is a bit in love with her. Five year old Pauli is the sunshine of the group.

The friends are a signed up team, mostly under Peter's leadership. They meet regularly after school and look for adventures.

One day Anya fails to turn up at the agreed meeting place. To begin with nobody thinks anything of it. She must have had something better to do, or else she's sick. When Paul asks her parents, however, and they have no idea where Anya is, the friends get worried. According to the parents, she went to school as usual. But none of the other children have seen her at all – it's very odd. Certainly she is impulsive, but simply not going to school and not telling anybody about it, that wouldn't be like her. "Let's hope nothing's happened to her," says Robert. "After all, Anya is a very pretty woman." Fortunately the implications of this are over Pauli's head. Andreas and Peter, on the other hand, imagine unpleasant scenarios. Andreas starts to analyze the situation. "Okay, we know she left home at 7:30, probably set out on the way to school and didn't arrive there. There's no indication of anything that might have happened to her." – "We have two possibilities," Peter goes on, "either we just wait and hope that she turns up again, or we look for further clues to her whereabouts."

"Wait!" Robert exclaims. "Wait?! Anya is in danger, and you talk of waiting? We must rescue her!" The friends decide to start their search on the path to school.

They walk the length of the school path and find nothing. They walk the path a second time, searching every bush, tree, thicket and bit of woodland to left and right. Again nothing!

The third time they do it, it is getting dark. Anya still hasn't turned up, and her parents have notified the police.

When the friends are following the path for one last time, now with little hope, an old, very grouchy looking woman comes to meet them. Pauli runs up to her beaming and unconcerned, and asks: "Have you seen Anya?" The old woman looks perplexed. Then she pulls her face into what is perhaps intended to be a smile, and answers: "The pretty blonde girl from this morning?" – "Yes," cries Peter, who has now joined them. "Have you seen her?"

"The Zardos took her," the old woman says. – "The Zardos? Whoever is that?" asks Robert, who has now also hurried up. The old woman starts laughing loudly, and doesn't stop. "Hey you!" Robert shouts. "Tell us this minute where we can find this Zardos, or I'll call the police." The old woman is still laughing, but she murmurs something that sounds like "In the mountains, behind the stone mask". The friends exchange questioning glances. When they look back at the old woman, she has disappeared – gone out like a light!

The same evening the friends resolve to search for the Zardos and the stone mask. Their parents, who have been told of the encounter, think the old woman must have been crazy, or just wanting to make herself interesting. But Andreas reflects: "How could the old woman have known that Anya was blonde?"

Next day the friends turn to the geography teacher, who is happy to help. He has a dim recollection that there is a rock formation in the mountains which the locals used to call the "stone mask". After some research in the school library, it proves possible to pinpoint the region. The friends write a letter to their parents and teachers, only to be opened that evening, telling them they are going to look for Anya. Their parents would never have allowed them to set off on this trip alone.

The mountain range where they are headed is a well developed skiing and hiking region. It is easy enough to get there. The stone mask is more difficult to find. Equipped with backpack, rope and tents, the friends traverse the region and climb one peak after another. The climbs become more and more exhausting. Andreas lectures them increasingly frequently, pointing out that the whole undertaking is completely illogical and senseless. Robert mutters to himself: "I hate that old woman. I should have killed her. If I told anyone what I'm doing here, they would have me committed at once." Peter too is asking by this time what the point of it all is. Even if they do find Anya, is she actually going to be alive? Shouldn't they have left the search to the professionals? On the other hand, what professional would be willing to look for her here in the mountains? Nobody could be that crazy. Does this Zardos exist at all? Did the old woman?

If it were not for Pauli, his irrepressible optimism and his unshakable faith, the friends would have given up. Give up? For Pauli, that would be the end of the world.

With reluctance – accompanied by feelings of obligation, guilt and anxiety, and the awareness that they are doing the right thing – and in a spirit of friendship and togetherness, they continue to search for Anya.

After a few days, they arrive at a rock face. Pauli exclaims: "There's the mask!" But all they can see is a cliff. Okay, with a good dose of imagination you could see the two caves in the wall as eyes, and the break line between them as a broken off nose. It's unlikely, but the others can't think of anything better either. And just at the point where, if it were a face, the mouth would be, the friends do indeed find, concealed between rocks, a wide, low cave entrance.

They follow the cave in, lighting the way with headlamps, and discover a stairway. The stair goes down and ends in an empty walled room. It is clear to them that they are not standing in a natural cave, but in an artificially created structure which is camouflaged by the rock face. A secret castle, built into the rock. Andreas turns quite pale: "If this castle exists, the Zardos must exist too." And Pauli adds, "Then Anya must be here as well."

Tense and nervous, the friends penetrate deeper into the complex. Every room and every passageway is different. Both the height, the size, the cut and even the levels of the rooms vary. Some chambers have windows, others small hatches or holes, some are pitch dark. They go up and down stairs, mostly following dark passageways. Everything is empty and painted white. No pictures, furniture or other objects, not a human soul. It is all uncannily still, with a disquieting atmosphere. The deeper the friends penetrate into this fastness, the darker and more confining it becomes. The sinister atmosphere becomes more oppressive all the time. They long since lost any idea of how to get back. And there's still no sign of Anya.

Gradually anxiety shifts into aggression. Robert loses his nerve, and shouts at the others: "We're all going to die! We're never getting out of here!" He gives Andreas a rude shove, and threatens Peter with his fist. Andreas yells back: "I warned you! It was crazy right from the start!" Before the situation can escalate, Peter comes between them. "We decided to do this together. Even Pauli was in favor!" – "Yes," says Andreas, stung, "we let ourselves be persuaded by a silly five year old child. Are we totally out of our minds?" Pauli starts to cry. – "I've had enough of this," says Robert, "I'm going back!" – "Good idea," Andreas agrees. "But what about Anya?" says Pauli in tearful tones. Robert replies emphatically, "It has become a matter of saving our own lives. Anya will just have to fend for herself."

"No!" Peter interrupts. "It's not about saving our lives, it's about our fear! What is threatening our lives here, apart from us?" There's an embarrassed silence... "We're going to see it through together. Never mind what happens. If we split up, we may never find each other again. Each of us has important skills. As solitary fighters we are weak and vulnerable."

Soon after this argument, the friends come to a deep dark shaft. Instinctively they feel that they must be quite close to the center.

They make the rope fast, and climb down. Deeper and deeper down. With every meter they climb, the air becomes colder and damper. When they reach the bottom, they can tell from the echo of their voices that they are standing in a gigantic hall. It is dark, uncanny and deathly quiet. Only the racing thud of their hearts can still be heard. They have to fight down their fear. On one side the hall ends in a natural cavern. Out of it emerges an ice cold breath of wind which moves lightly over their skin. They can sense for certain that something dreadful, something desperately dangerous, something evil is lurking in that cave. Let's not go any farther! Don't let yourselves be seen!

All the same, the friends venture a few more steps into the cave. In a nook they see a transparent wall, pulsing with a dim red and white light. A faint low pitched wheezing can be heard. Behind this wall – that's where it is. It's evil. Pure evil. The Zardos!

Their fear escalates into panic. Their legs hurt, and just want to run away! Their arms tremble, they tremble all over. They only have one thought left: run away, as fast as you possibly can!

Peter struggles for control. The friends take hands, and slowly walk backwards, as quietly as possible, into the hall. Peter takes another look around, and notices a heavy iron door. The door opens. To his vast astonishment, it leads directly into the open air. From this point he can look over the valley. Armed with this knowledge, he now really pulls himself together and resolves to confront the Zardos. Once again they take hands, and advance resolutely on the pulsing shimmering wall. Again they start to tremble. The fear is insupportable. "If it discovers us, it won't just kill us, it will steal our souls," Peter thinks. At the same time he feels a kind of fascination. This is pure evil. It calls for absolute surrender, abandonment of all responsibilities. Just be a victim.

Before the friends reach the shimmering wall, they are startled by steps coming from behind them. Very tense, they turn instantly and see a group of young people, who have also descended the shaft. Clearly they too want to see the Zardos. The friends conceal themselves, and observe what happens. The newcomers creep forward, their knees trembling, toward the shimmering wall.

They are fearful and fascinated. Their shallow breathing and thudding heartbeats can be heard. Their eyes glitter in the light coming from the wall. Suddenly one of them yells, like one possessed, "It's coming! It's coming!" And they all run for their lives. As if the devil were after them they scatter, each of them vanishing into some dark passageway. As the sound of their footfalls dies away, the deathly silence returns.

Something is happening to the shimmering wall. The light becomes brighter, and the wall opens a crack. The friends hold their breath. In the crack, a creature that seems to be human appears. It is wearing a big white mask with a terrifying expression, suggesting images of the gods from ancient times.

It's Zardos.

Zardos doesn't seem anything like as evil and dangerous as they were expecting. He seems surprised to find the friends suddenly standing there in front of him. "Oh, I didn't think there was still anybody here," the creature says with a clear, youthful sounding voice. The friends are still frozen with terror. Peter asks quietly: "Are you Evil?"

"Yes," Zardos answers. "I am the mirror for the fear and the evil that dwell in you. I show you your own dark side, and the fascination that evil exercises on you. I make you feel your fear, feel yourselves, feel your lives. I make you sense the risk of losing everything, and the fascination that the idea of losing everything has for you. I show you what must not be allowed to happen. I am what you don't want to see in yourselves."

The friends look down at the floor, silent and confused. After a while Peter asks with concern: "Where is Anya?"

"She was here," Zardos replies. "She wanted to see me, but then she made off through the iron door. Now you will have to excuse me please, I must go back, the next group is already coming down the shaft." In the distance they can hear people climbing down the shaft, determined to confront their terror.

The friends leave the castle by way of the iron door. Relieved to be back in the "normal" world, they consider where they should look for Anya. "If I know Anya," Peter says, "she'll go up a mountain if she's scared." There's a cable car going up the mountain. All the same, the friends proceed on foot, not wanting to miss Anya whatever they do. After a march lasting several hours, they come to a little hut by a mountain station. Anya is sitting on a bench in front of it, freezing, huddled over and terrified. When she sees her friends, it's like a sunrise. They throw their arms around one another, kissing and hugging. Now everything is OK. They are back together again, complete again. Even Robert, who was on the point of telling her off in round terms, can only say how happy and thankful he is.

In the hut they get something to eat and drink, and Anya tells them what happened to her.

"On the way to school I met an old woman. I was scared, and gave her a wide berth. The old woman challenged me, and asked what I was afraid of. 'There are plenty of bad and dangerous people in the world,' I answered, 'and you make me a bit nervous. I haven't ever seen you here before.' The old woman laughed – she liked my honesty – and said the only really dangerous thing was my own fears. If I wouldn't face up to my fears, they would determine my whole life. They would force me to serve them, and them alone. I would try to tell myself that my actions were necessary and reasonable, that I had no other choice, that my responsibilities demanded this course of action or that, that I mustn't be bad, that I must be dependable and so on. But in truth my decisions would not be taken in the light of external circumstances, out of my own insights or inward needs, but only out of fear. I just wasn't aware of it.

"I asked the old woman, 'How can I tell when I'm acting out of fear, and when it is on reasonable grounds or for good reason?' – 'You mustn't fight your fear or drive it away,' the old woman said, 'but embrace it like a friend – then it will show its true colors, then it will reveal itself openly and honestly. You can be grateful to it, you can see it as a friend, without letting yourself be manipulated or dominated by it. Your fear has protected you, of course, in many dangerous situations. I will take you to the Zardos. He will show you how to encounter your fear and accept it.'

"The old woman, who was a witch I guess, flew me with her broom to the mountain with the stone mask, and put me down in front of the iron door. I went in.

"When I faced the illuminated wall, something seemed to be moving behind it. Deadly fear and panic took hold of me, and I ran out through the iron door into the open. I didn't find in myself the courage to face him and embrace him. Now I have the feeling that he's going to be following me my whole life long."

"That doesn't surprise me," says Robert. "A weak girl is bound to be frightened." – "Just that is the illusion," Peter interposes. "Robert, you are less fearful, because you think you are strong. But to Zardos strength, cleverness and experience are all irrelevant. Every individual, even if they are unaware of it, is contending with themselves. Zardos is your mirror image. Can you be stronger, faster or more skillful than your mirror image or your shadow? Who's going to win? It's always going to be you. Who's going to lose? Again, it's always going to be you. Everyone has the same chances. Now Anya needs to look for another way of embracing her fear, and so embracing herself. Otherwise she won't be able to live a life of freedom."

First of all the friends return to their village, where they are welcomed with joyful relief.

The narrow path

Life has now returned to its normal channels. But Anya keeps herself to herself, and is increasingly subdued. Her health suffers as well. She has headaches and stomach aches, dizzy attacks, a racing heart and diarrhea – all these keep her in bed a lot. Her former cheerfulness and optimism seem to have vanished completely. She is anxious, sad and lacking in self esteem. Sudden noises frighten her to death; she no longer leaves the house, and strange people make her paralytically nervous. Her friends are desperate. All their affection, their injunctions and words of advice seem fruitless. The doctors too are totally at a loss. In their desperation, the friends decide to look for the witch who started it all. But how do you find a witch? Nobody seems to know the old woman.

After lengthy analysis and discussion, the friends finally come to the conclusion that the witch was not visiting just by chance – something must have summoned her. But what can this have been, and why should it have led her steps to Anya, of all people? Didn't she foretell to Anya exactly what has happened since? But why Anya, that cheerful, happy-go-lucky girl?

Unusual questions call for unusual answers. So the friends decide to visit a person in the village who is likewise highly unusual, and generally avoided. They go to the key maker. The key maker isn't just responsible for locks on doors, and so for domestic security – he is also a kettle mender, scissors grinder, artistic blacksmith, creative spirit and an adviser in all life situations. Dark of skin, he moved to the village from Africa some twenty years ago – an alien and a shaman from an alien culture. The villagers treat him with nervous respect and with mistrust. Some visit him in secret, to get his helpful advice for problems with their partner or with their neighbors, or other causes of dissension. He is thought to be a wise and spiritual man, and is also thought to have healing powers.

With great seriousness and a gloomy expression, the key maker hears Anya's story. Then he says, "The witch wanted to help Anya, but she did the opposite and brought her bad luck. Instead of getting Anya to find the Zardos of her own volition and on her own resources, she just carried her there directly. As a result, Anya's path of development was curtailed and cut loose from the natural order of things. Now she needs to cover the ground that was missed out. This is only possible with the help of a ritual, which calls for a lot of courage. The candidate must be prepared to risk his or her life. Ask Anya if she is willing to perform this ritual, and what she is willing to sacrifice."

After lengthy discussion, Anya decides to give it a go. Of course the friends have put together a considerable amount of cash to pay the key maker. But they are all aware that some other kind of sacrifice will be required.

The friends accompany Anya to the place indicated by the shaman for the ritual. It's a remote place in the woods, by a small pond. The key maker shows up in a shamanistic costume of furs and colored ribbons, ornamented with bones, driftwood, pearls, animals' teeth and birds' claws. He also carries a bag full of incense and incense materials, colored powders, rattles, bells and a drum. He is painted all over, and looks very mysterious, as if he had come from a different planet. The friends are reluctant to leave Anya alone with the shaman. But it must be done. The ritual is meant only for Anya. She has to tread this path without their support.

First of all, the key maker purifies the place with smudging, and with strange symbols and signs that he scratches in the ground. He draws a circle around the place of the ritual with his colored powders. He and Anya both drink a bitter tasting drink, and dance to the drum. It is dark by this time, and the place is dimly lit with torches. After something like two hours of dancing and mantric intoning in a strange and incomprehensible language, the shaman starts painting Anya with colors and mysterious symbols. She has to take her clothes off and let herself be smeared with a stinking ointment. She feels hot and dizzy. She begins to sweat, her skin is crawling all over. The noises of the woodland, the drumming and the singing of the shaman become louder. The light of the torches casts wild, sinister shadows which dance among the bushes and the trees. Suddenly a cat with glowing eyes emerges from the thicket, and comes towards her. "Come with me, I will show you the way," the cat says. As if in a trance, Anya gets up, takes a torch and follows the cat into the woods. Soon after, the two of them are facing the entrance to a cave. "From here," the cat says, "you must continue on your own. This is the entrance to a labyrinth, your life path. On your way to the center you will encounter dangers and challenges which will be your teachers. Be without fear, and trust your intuition and your heart."

Firmly resolved not to run away this time, Anya summons up all her courage and enters the cave. After a few meters, the passageway becomes so low and so narrow that she has to lie flat and crawl. The ground of the passage is cold damp clay. "Not stony at least, thank God," Anya thinks. It is almost impossible to pay attention to the ceiling, the walls and the floor simultaneously, so as to avoid bumps and scratches. With only slight hurts she negotiates the narrow passage and emerges into a wider corridor. Now it is a stony floor, and walking barefoot is painful. Sometimes rocks block the path, and she has to get around or over them. While Anya is focused on the path, she notices shadows on the walls out of the corner of her eye. Has something moved, behind those stone walls? She panics, and cowers anxiously behind a boulder. "So I'm not alone here? That's dreadful. I'm completely naked and without protection. If I shout, nobody is going to hear me. Whatever am I going to do?"

For a few minutes it is absolutely still. Then Anya is hit by a pebble. The next pebble misses her narrowly. She hears somebody tittering. She pulls herself together and calls, "Who are you? Come out! I saw you!" But there is no answer.

Then something moves behind a rock. A little girl in a white First Communion dress appears. She climbs on the rocks, laughs naughtily and sticks out her tongue at Anya. Anya is so surprised that she forgets her fear, stands up and asks, "How did you get here?" – "Don't say that!" the laughing girl replies. "Come on, old thing, let's play hide and seek." As if by reflex, Anya is about to say, "Oh, I love that!" – but then it occurs to her that she isn't a child any longer, she is on a quest and she shouldn't be playing with children in her present state. If the child's parents were to show up, just imagine how embarrassing that would be! So she replies: "I don't want to play games. But how did you get here? Are you frightened, here in the dark?" – "Frightened? Of you? You do look pretty dirty, but I like you all the same," the girl says. "Your dress is fabulous. I'd like to have one like that myself!" Anya looks down at herself and sees that she is so coated with earth and clay that in the torchlight it really looks like a closely fitting dress. She smiles: "There's no need to be afraid of me, but why are you here all alone? Where are your parents?" – "I don't know," the girl replies, but then she is distracted by a noise. Out of the darkness a ram appears. "Well, what do you know, I want to give him a stroke! Come on!" the girl exclaims with excitement. She and Anya follow the somewhat malodorous animal further into the cave.

The entrance to the cave reverses direction, and seems to be taking them back on their tracks. From the passage there emerge the clear notes of a flute. They echo off the walls. Ghostly, lonely and lost – that is the impression the melodies leave. The ram accelerates its pace. Anya turns to the girl, but she has disappeared. Anya calls out, and goes back some distance, but there is no trace of the girl. Finally she gives up searching, and follows the flute music. At the end of the passage there is bright firelight. Here sits a pretty boy, about her own age, playing the flute with feeling. Close by the ram is tethered. It's like a painting from the Romantic era, only even more naff. Anya, now feeling braver and naughtier, approaches the evidently anxious boy and asks, "Who are you?" – The boy drops his flute on the floor, utters a cry and runs away as if he has seen a ghost. Anya can't help having a good laugh. Surely she doesn't look as bad as that? But suddenly it occurs to her that there might be more to it. She turns slowly round...

And finds herself facing a dragon with fiery eyes and hot breath. She wants to run, but her legs won't respond. She falls to the ground. The dragon launches itself, hissing. It jumps right over Anya, and seizes the complaining ram in its jaws. At the moment when the dragon is above her, Anya has a strange feeling of relief, almost a feeling of happiness – as if at the moment of greatest danger fear has completely deserted her. Sometimes fear is just a mist wraith. From a distance it looks gigantic and insuperable, but the closer you come, the smaller and more "fearful" it becomes.

Having finished its meal, the dragon looks round at Anya. "What are you waiting for?" he spits, in a deep minatory voice. "Jump on, we need to get going." Anya's sense of rationality waves a white flag and surrenders. Without her willing it, her body gets up quite of its own accord, races forward and jumps on the dragon's back. The dragon grunts with satisfaction, and flexes his muscles slightly. She senses a vibration between her thighs, which pervades the body of the dragon and her own – as if a 2000 HP engine has been started, but being still in neutral has not yet sprung into action. The dragon shouts, "Hold on tight!!" Anya clings to his back and holds on as tightly as she can. The dragon's muscles tense and become as hard as steel. With a jerk that could have come from a steam hammer, the powerhouse accelerates. After a few steps the dragon spreads its wings, mounts sharply and flies through a big hole in the cave ceiling. Anya feels so closely connected with the dragon, it is as if they are one being. She feels mighty and invincible.

Nothing can stop her. Liberated, she laughs and shouts with all her might to express her gladness, while the warm wind rushes through her hair and around her body. Has she ever been so happy before?

The dragon, who has picked up on Anya's exuberant feelings, loops the loop, folds his wings and goes into a nosedive. Then he says, "Now you know what flying is like. Your turn now. Fly with me." Anya sits upright, spreads her arms out and sees that the wings of the dragon move in response to her arm movements – as if their nerves are connected, and she is controlling the body of the dragon. She senses the untamed power and energy, the fire, the destructive violence and rage of the creature – but also the unconditional love of life, of nature and human beings. Only one thing the dragon has no knowledge of – fear! Sensing his own power, how could he be afraid?

Anya, the invincible, now wants to know everything. Below her is a deep blue lake. She goes into a nosedive and plunges into the water. The impact is painful, and she shoots like an arrow, deeper and deeper, down to the bottom. When they touched down she lost the dragon, and now finds herself alone in the dark depths. It's strange – although the dragon is no longer to be seen or sensed, she still feels connected with him. She doesn't panic, but tries to get her bearings in the water, feeling confident and curious. In one direction a dim light can be made out. As she approaches it, the light turns out to be a little underwater city, surrounded by an air bubble.

She enters the city through a kind of airlock, and finds herself in the thick of things immediately. Everyone is running around with no clothes on, just like her. But most of them have belts of seaweed, rag cloths, jewelry made of pearls and precious metals and other kinds of ornaments. It's a strange, bright, alien world. These creatures look like human beings, though they have web skin between their fingers and toes. Their noses and ears close with flaps of skin. Their eyes are twice as big as human eyes. They have scales in some places.

When the creatures catch sight of Anya, they throw themselves to the ground in terror. Groveling on the ground, they moan and yammer: "Please spare our lives, great empress! We are your unworthy servants. Honorable mistress, speak and it shall be performed!" Life in the city has suddenly come to a stop. As far as her eye can see, all the inhabitants are kneeling to her. A quiet anxious murmuring fills the air. Anya looks cautiously round. Perhaps the empress is standing right behind her. But no, evidently they are referring to her. Confused, and wondering whether it may all be a dream, she says, "My good people, there seems to be some mistake. You don't know me!" An elderly resident, wearing an exceptional number of ornaments – he must be a high placed official – falls on his knees in front of her: "How could we not know your majesty? In your majesty's absence, we have kept everything as you would wish. At last you are back, great empress. If your majesty will please follow me. Ever since you left, the palace has been kept ready for your return."

In the old days Anya would have done everything in her power to avoid being elevated to a position like this. Never would she have dared take responsibility for a city and all its inhabitants. How can she fulfill the tasks of government and meet people's expectations? She's just a young woman with average schooling, and now she's suddenly supposed to be an empress? When the truth comes out, she will surely be beheaded on the spot (that being the usual method of execution for persons of rank). But her dragon blood reminds her of her power. What is there to be afraid of?

In the palace she is received as befits her station. She is dressed in luxurious drapes and the most expensive jewelry. A host of servants, soldiers, guards and counselors assure her of their loyalty and swear their obedience unto death.

But the balance of power is not so stable as it appears. On the very next day, guards tell her that some counselors are planning a revolution, with the aim of seizing power for themselves. She must watch out for assassins, saboteurs and terrorists, strengthen the watch and give the guards special emergency powers. Ideally she should not leave the palace at all, or only with the army or an escort to protect her. The counselors, for their part, warn her that a rumor is going around that she is not the empress but an impostor. Now some elements in the army have turned against her and are meditating revolt. Anya is desperate. Everybody is turning against her. Everyone wants to get rid of her, and is identified only with their own interests. Evidently at the time she disappeared the position of empress was a great deal stronger and more secure than has since become. Now she represents just a target, a projection screen for the appetites, wishes and demands of every single member of the population. "Your humble servants" – are you kidding me? They just want me to serve their own ends! It makes Anya furious, and she rages through the palace. Of course dragons are quite capable of breathing fire.

But what is she going to do? Dismiss everyone who might turn out to be a security risk? She can't do that. There are just too many of them. If her enemies join in a conspiracy against her, her reign will soon be over. Should she resort to standard political maneuvers? Encourage interest groups and play them off against each other, give certain groups positions and perquisites to keep them sweet, foment popular anxiety so as to make herself indispensable and play the role of a protector, select scapegoats and persecute minorities, stir up unrest and wars to destabilize the social order? But this kind of thing doesn't appeal. Such measures would lead to conflict among the inhabitants. It would be the end of peace.

In the night she asks the dragon for help. In a dream, she gets the following advice:

"Power forces those who serve it to be powerless. For the will to power makes the willing the slave of its own logic. So get rid of power. How?
Get rid of powerlessness, and power too disappears.
What gets rid of powerlessness?
Responsibility and freedom!
One who wishes to change an existing power structure, doesn't need to replace the old players with new ones; he must transfer responsibility and authority to the existing players."

On the following morning the empress summons her court, soldiers, guards and counselors and makes a public address. In her speech she calls on persons in prominent positions by name, thanks them for all they have done to date and offers some of them new tasks, responsibilities, authority and competences, spelling it all out in detail. Every citizen should know exactly the limits of their competence and what they are responsible for, so it is clear who can be called to account or rewarded. There will always be critics, smart alecks and revolutionaries. And that's OK. They bring improvements and new ideas, they renew and stabilize society. They deserve to be given a hug for their loving service.

The speech is a complete success. Something shifts in the city. It's a breath of fresh air, a new mood of hope.

That evening Anya is on the point of withdrawing to her apartments, when a man with a white mask appears. "May I introduce myself," he says. "I am Zardos. We've met before. You are little Anya, who ran away from me." Anya looks at him with surprise and alarm. Suddenly she feels she is just a weak little girl again, and stammers, "Yes, that's me. But how did you get here? What do you want?" – "The witch sent me to get you," Zardos answers. "Do you want to spend the rest of your life as an empress in a giant air bubble? You haven't got to the center of the labyrinth yet."

Anya feels hot and cold. Where is her dragon energy, what has become of the revered empress and ruler of an entire city? Some guy comes along who doesn't even dare to show his face, tells her that once upon a time she used to be small and timorous, and she just collapses! Her initial apprehension converts to rage. Perhaps that dragon blood hasn't disappeared after all. "Okay," she says. "I used to be very frightened. But that is a thing of the past. Let's see what kind of metal you are made of. We're going back to your cave together."

A typically childish reaction of defiance, you may well think, dear reader – but how would you have reacted? What would your heart have said?

Anya summons her servants and tells them to prepare for her departure. The same evening a fish taxi – a small whale, in whose maw two persons can sit comfortably – takes Anya and Zardos through an intricate and extensive underwater cave system back to the labyrinth, where Anya's journey began.

All this time not a word has been exchanged. Only when they have firm ground under their feet, and are standing in the cave passage does Zardos ask, "Don't you want to light a torch?" – Anya asks, "Why? Are you scared?" – No answer. – "Okay," says Zardos finally, "so we'll manage without a light. It's your cave."

The two feel their way along the wall. After just a few meters, the passage turns through a hundred and eighty degrees. The walls have sharper edges, the floor gets increasingly slippery and stalactites block their path. Zardos, who goes first, curses under his breath with increasing frequency, because he has bumped or scratched something. Anya too has taken a few knocks. Of course she doesn't say anything.

Suddenly Zardos gives a loud panicky yell. The cry penetrates her to the marrow. Anya is shocked, and a moment later she hears a dull thud. Then it is deathly quiet. She lights a torch, and sees to her horror that she is standing on the brink of a deep precipice. The path runs directly along the edge, and gets narrower and more slippery all the time. Very cautiously she moves to the edge and shines the torch into the depths. A few meters down, Zardos is lying motionless on a rocky outcrop. "For God's sake, whatever am I going to do now?" Crazy thoughts shoot through her head in confusion. On the one hand she feels she is to blame, because she didn't want to light a torch; at the same time she can't deny that Zardos' discomfiture gives her a certain satisfaction. Such schadenfreude, of course, is inappropriate and unacceptable. "There's a person down there, or whatever he is, seriously injured or maybe even dead. I must help! But how? If only I had a rope or a ladder. But as it is, I could never get down. I hate this kind of guy. First he makes me look stupid, then he gives me a guilty conscience!"

Anya sits on the edge of the precipice arguing with herself over the unfortunate situation. A low moaning reaches her ears: "Please help me! Help!" Anya's heart contracts. Now she really needs to be strong and intelligent. She just can't do anything for Zardos. Any attempt to rescue him would be suicidal.

The wind rises. An icy breath blows from the abyss. The cold penetrates her to the marrow of her bones. She trembles in every limb, feels empty and depleted. Out of the depth of the abyss a billow of smoke approaches – no, it is a ghostly form, barely to be made out, with a skull. "Anya," breathes a whispering voice, "Anya, come with me. I will deliver you! I can give you peace! It's all going to be all right." In her desperation Anya cries, "Dragon! Please help me! Help!" The ghostly being laughs. "Your dragon is busy." Zardos' groans become louder, echoing from the walls of the cave. Other voices are mingled with the groaning. First they are a long way away, then the voices become clearer and louder. "Anya! Anya! Turn round! Come back!" – "Peter? Andreas? Robert? Pauli? Where are you? Come here, I need your help." She has a glimmer of hope that her friends may show up at once. Then everything would be OK. But her hope is dashed. The friends call: "We can't get to you. You must come to us. Turn round! Go back!"

"I can't do that!" Anya calls. "I can't just leave everything here and go!" What is she going to do? Increasingly desperate, she looks at the skull and thinks, "I must make a decision. A decision without compromise, without consideration of advantage or disadvantage, ignoring danger, reason and the expectations and interests of others. A decision that is simply and solely my decision, which feels right for me, which my heart approves. Only that way can I find peace."

Anya feels her way to the edge of the precipice, and jumps.

She lands on the rocky projection, right next to Zardos. Although she has no idea how she is ever going to get down from here, she feels relieved – as if a massive weight has been taken off her shoulders. She sheds tears, kneels down by Zardos and gives him a loving hug. At the same moment she is surrounded by dense smoke. She has a fit of coughing. When the smoke withdraws, she is kneeling on the bank of the little pond with the key maker and hugging herself. Zardos has disappeared. The key maker looks at her kindly, stands up, packs his tools away and leaves. Anya waits till the sun rises. Then she too packs up her things, gets dressed and goes home to her new life.

The Storm

The storm drives me before it.

For it I am an obstacle,

a check to its flow.

Its world is different from mine,

intentionless, true and undivided.

I meet him and us

in this otherworld,

but we are at home on different planets.

I seek togetherness,

seek its love

and find my longing.

Were I wind,

I would be true,

would be flowing,

we would be one.

This is a story of storms, a story of the seas, and a story of those who come to me to appease their longing. It is also my story.

Since I was born, I have been looking out to sea. Looking out at the curved horizon which makes the water flow in waves to the coast, which swallows the colors of the sky before they rejoin the sun.

I have always lived on the beach. The rushing of the wind, the up-and-down of the surf have accustomed my sight and hearing to a rhythm, to the constant reminder that I should be a part of the forces of nature.

My little cottage is built on wooden piles in the dunes. As the only son of a fishing family, I lead a solitary existence. Father is out at sea all day, Mother sells smoked fish in the distant village. My parents' life is strenuous, unspectacular and monotonous. But they are happy and contented. Actually I am also contented, but I feel something drawing me out into the world. There are so many things I do not understand or know, so many adventures and challenges out there! – which I, in my overweening confidence, would of course handle effortlessly.

Then SHE comes along, and there is no more holding me back. She travels through the world like a bird of passage, without any fear of the massive distances or the dangers, always having a distant goal in view. For me she is the archetype of freedom, independence and self-confidence. Her roots do not grow in the earth of my homeland, but in the soul. The soul knows no places to which it need be bound.

Courage is the wrong word. You need courage when you are afraid. She is carefree. Bad things happen to her so that she can learn from them. Life gives her pain so that she can experience intense happiness. You can't have the one without the other. She doesn't waste precious time on self-limitation and fantasies of making things last. Everything in her life is in motion, everything is storm and she lets herself be driven by it – in intentionless power and resonance.

95

To begin with it was just curiosity. We rented a room for holiday visitors, and she moved in for three days. I offered to show her the locality. The most beautiful bay, the oldest tree, the most magnificent view. She smiled her assent, and without knowing the reason, I felt relieved.

She is so different, but nonetheless in resonance with me. Even without words. As the wind stirs the sea, so she stirs my stillness and my longing. For three days we plunge into our open hearts, and treat the still unhealed wounds with the breath of love and sympathy.

With her tenderness she makes me resonate, so I am enveloped and protected by my vulnerable being like a newborn child. These three days are an entire lifetime. A life outside the familiar rules of play, out of time and out of place.

After her, the knowledge remains that there is much more life out there – more light, more intensive, more authentic experience. After her, I feel different. I will never be me again. I have been re-engendered, and must now come to birth. Part migrating bird, part strand of the sea have given birth to me. Now I leave the egg and fly to unknown countries, to the powers that will cast me into the sea, to the pains that will disempower me. I will live what I STILL am. My death will be just one episode in my existence, a small and insignificant one…

Now I am living in the town. Here too I look out to sea – a sea of people and walls. Masses of people move through the streets, apparently aimless, planless, monotone. As if they were trying to be a herd, as inconspicuous and anonymous as possible – a herd where all act as if they had a place and a job to do, in some mysterious scheme of things. But the impression deceives, as everything here deceives. What connects these people is the place, and the function of "consuming" it. Anticipation of the moment of supposed possession, of supposed acknowledgement, of one's own pride and conceited admiration. The comparison with others, and valuation of everything, are what drives them. The hope to live better than others, the fear to live worse than others, these are their constant companions. Consumption needs others, needs crowds of people. On a desert island, the craziness of this would be obvious at once. In the town, on the other hand, natural forces do not prevail. The town is dominated by dream worlds, the fantasies and illusions of a judging and evaluating society.

Who are we in the crowd? Who are we as individuals?

I am individual, but not alone. I belong to the group made up of all individuals, and am like all the others. I am heavily preoccupied loneliness, loneliness that distracts from itself. The more people I meet, the more appointments I keep, the stronger becomes my hunger for togetherness.
What dish makes you full for ever?
Love? Sympathy? Gratitude? Devotion?
Or their opposites?

Are these the coins we are supposed to pay with?
Should I pay the price?
Will it cost me the loss of myself?
What remains of me, if I lose myself?

The storm and the sea tear the coast away, to create new land somewhere else. The surrendered self does not disappear, it creates new beaches, a new life, in movement, in resonance with the wind and the sea, eternally rising and falling, harmoniously connected with everything, together with everything.

The feeling of being alive arises through conscious change, in harmony with everything. The greater the change, the more magnificent the harmony.

Were I to play the new melody of life,
I would recreate my being,
would be storm,
would be flow,
would be happy,
would be one.

The Hakomies

In a distant country there lives a group of elves on an island in the middle of a big lake. This peaceful tribe of elves has a population of just forty. They live remote from the world, and are completely self-supporting on their inconspicuous isle.

They call themselves the Hakomies. Fishing, fruits of the forest and little fields of vegetables, potatoes and spelt are enough to keep them going. Along with their gentle disposition and emotional equanimity, the Hakomies have a very special ability – they can get in touch with each other telepathically. When in a meditative state, they can exchange thoughts and feelings with one another over any distance.

The tribe is headed by a chieftain, Alo. In making decisions, Alo takes advice from the medicine man Achack and from Pavati, the wise old woman. The members of the tribe all enjoy equal rights and equal status. Each of them carries out their job, as a part of this closely knit community. Though they each have their own reed huts, they get together every morning for breakfast, and every evening for the evening meal on the village square. This is an occasion for announcing and discussing new happenings, and sorting out any disputes and unpleasantnesses, with Alo acting as arbiter. For generations the elves have been leading a simple life, but a contented and happy one, in the seclusion of their island.

Then one day something very unusual happens. Something that old tales tell of. Nobody ever really believed that such things could have happened in the past, or that they could actually recur in the present.

The day starts like any other day. The sun is shining, it's a pleasant quiet morning. There's an uncanny stillness over the country. The animals fall silent, and there is a deathly hush… Unbearable tension is felt in the air. Babies start to cry, and women hide in their huts.

.

After a few minutes, the earth begins to shake. The ground rocks like the deck of a ship. Every shift of the soil makes you lose your fundamental belief in the abiding solidity of the ground under your feet. You feel a rising fear of being swallowed up by the earth. In the past there have been earth tremors, but this is on a wholly unprecedented scale. After five powerful jolts, it seems to be all over.

All the people meet on the village square, in agitation. A few women are weeping, and a some of the men have brought weapons with them. Achak and Pavati focus on those who seem fearful and confused, trying to calm them as best they can. Finally Alo makes himself heard above the tumult, by banging loudly on the dinner gong. "Quiet! Quiet!" he shouts. "Listen to me! It's over! Check to see if anyone is missing and what damage has been done."

Calls from the distance reach the village square on the wind. "The lake! The lake! It's disappearing!" One of the fishermen comes running as fast as he can, and shouts again, "The lake is disappearing! It's going down!" Alo, Achak and Pavati exchange glances. Then, as if by agreement, they set off simultaneously, making swiftly for the bank of the lake. The others follow them.

It's a fact! The water has already withdrawn some fifty meters from the shore, and the bottom of the lake shows bare. Visibly upset and perturbed, Alo announces that he will withdraw to take counsel with Achak and Pavati.

The three of them spend several hours in the hut of the medicine man, performing rituals. Meanwhile the water level continues to fall rapidly. As if a dam has been broken, the water rushes in gigantic whirlpools into deep cracks in the earth.

Fish are twitching and dying everywhere, and there is a stench of rottenness and corruption. The Hakomies stand in horror on the bank, and simply can't believe what they are seeing.

So it goes on until the late evening. Only after the shared evening meal does village life gradually get moving again. Going through their accustomed routines seems to restore the Hakomies' self-confidence and sense of security. They all assemble on the village square. This time no cheerful laughter or voices of playing children can be heard, there is just a subdued murmur. Finally Alo appears from the hut, followed by the medicine man and the wise woman. They take up their position in front of the tables.

"My dear people," Alo says in firm tones, "we are faced with a severe trial. A trial that will show whether we can hold onto our courage for life, our confidence in our own abilities, our ideals and principles, our faith, our roots and our identity. Everything is going to change. Our former means of subsistence, fishing, is no longer possible. The defense against enemies that the water gave us in the past is gone. We are no longer on an island. We are no longer alone. Now we must expect to be faced with dangers and enemies. Our destiny lies in the hands of the All-One. It is up to us to make something of the task it has set us."

In the following days the Hakomies are busy making preparations to deal with their new situation. They consider whether small parties should make their way across to the mainland in order to hunt, or whether it would be better to convert to a purely vegetarian diet. No member of the tribe is an experienced hunter. Apart from birds, no large animals have been living on the island. For the moment they decide to rely exclusively on a vegetarian diet. But three fishermen say they are willing to explore the mainland and learn how to hunt.

On the mainland there live the Sakiras, a tribe of elves with a population of over a thousand. Very soon the inexperienced and rather clueless fishermen are discovered and captured by the Sakiras, and led before their chieftain. The fishermen willingly explain why they are here, and what has happened to their people. They expect the Sakiras to have sympathy for their plight and help them. But the Sakiras treat them with scorn and contempt, beat them and lock them in a cage.

The life of the Sakiras is characterized above all by competitiveness, and by the struggle for power and riches. So naturally they are all in competition with one another. The most highly regarded persons among them are the most powerful ones, the most cunning and the richest.

The chief of the Sakiras consults his minister of war at once, and plans a campaign against the Hakomies. The very next morning, their hundred best warriors take arms and march across what used to be the lake to the island.

The Hakomies see the warriors coming while they are still far away, and despair. They have nothing to set against this military force. For a handful of farmers and fisherfolk, a battle with a hundred experienced fighters would be completely hopeless. So Alo decides, with a heavy heart, to take Achak and go to meet the attackers, with a view to surrendering. Perhaps they can arrive at a peaceful solution. In the Sakiras' eyes, surrender is a dishonorable and cowardly act. They kill Alo und Achak on the spot, march into the village, kill children, rape, pillage and set huts on fire.

This day – the darkest day the Hakomies have ever experienced – will go down in history. The suffering, pain and despair are immeasurable. It is a nightmare that burns deeply into the soul.

The Sakiras make slaves of the survivors, and take them back to their village. Here a slave market has already been made ready. The captured fishermen are sold to farmers as field workers.

As the warriors parade triumphantly through the streets with their prisoners, they are frenetically cheered by jubilant and ecstatic crowds. When they reach the market place, a feast is already in full swing. The booty is scrutinized and the Hakomies are shown off like exotic animals. The ensuing sale proceeds apace. High prices are paid in some cases. The Hakomies are a noble and handsome people. Even the ancient Pavati finds a buyer, being purchased by a historical author for secretarial tasks.

For the Hakomies, this is the start of a fearful time. They have never had to serve anyone or obey orders before. They have always been independent, free, proud elves, living on their own responsibility. Now begins a time of violence, humiliation and oppression. They are the victims of fate. From now on the Sakiras determine whether the Hakomies live or die. They decide who is right and who is wrong, who is beautiful or ugly, good or bad, lazy or diligent. They dictate who belongs to whom, who ranks higher or lower. Their estimates determine the value of a Hakomie and the price that must be paid in order to own one.

The one secret remaining to the Hakomies is their telepathic ability. In the past this ability was taken so much for granted that they never needed to talk about it. Now it emerges how special and valuable this talent is, for their survival and for sustaining the sense of togetherness. By this time they are also smart enough to keep this secret to themselves, and so avoid it falling into the power of the Sakiras. Every morning at four the Hakomies wake up, and get in touch with each other telepathically. This connection gives them comfort and hope.

Their enslavement, their emotional and physical pain and helplessness inflict deep wounds. In the course of time, the thinking and feeling of the Hakomies starts to alter. It is a creeping development, but a lasting one.

Pavati, who has emerged as the spiritual leader of the tribe, is the first to notice it. She has made it her task, during these telepathic sessions, to bring order to the mental and emotional chaos of the others, and to create an open dialog space where all have an equal say. During the sessions she notices that the thinking of the elves is progressively changing. They identify more and more with the judgments, assessments and values of the Sakiras and with the roles the Sakiras have allotted to them. The Hakomies now feel themselves to be worthless slaves. They are afraid of punishment, compete with one another, lie, hurt each other, strive for reward, try to be pleasing to their tormentors in order to reap benefits, nurture violent and aggressive fantasies, harbor desires for revenge and so on.

It becomes more and more difficult for Pavati to convey and preserve the original identity and the values of the Hakomies. As increasing numbers of the Hakomies have adopted the thoughts and values of the Sakiras, their situation seems to them all the more desperate and miserable. Some try to improve things by obedience and devotion to their masters, others resort to opposition and resistance. They sabotage the Sakiras at every opportunity, and try to sow discord. Neither course improves their position. The obedient ones are exploited all the more, and the truculent are punished increasingly severely, in some cases even executed.

By this time most of the Hakomies have completely given up their old ideals and values, and take their cue just from the Sakiras. As a result they grow dissatisfied with Pavati as their leader and with the old code of behavior, and want to change things. They forge plans for violent liberation from their slavery. But every time, when these plans come down to the level of detail, they have to admit that their can't do anything against the might of the Sakiras. There are too many of them, and they are too good at fighting. What can a handful of slaves do? They will always remain in bondage, and can only bend to circumstances. They adapt as well as they can to their fate, and hope for a miracle, a great leader or some kind of redemption to come. Perhaps in the world hereafter they will be rewarded for their suffering.

Gradually they even take on the religious beliefs of the Sakiras. These are based on reward and punishment. It is a faith that promises redemption from suffering and a paradise after death. Apparently the more suffering you have had in life, the greater your reward in the hereafter. For slaves, this is a comforting thought.

Even their new faith cannot altogether blot out their memories of a happy past, or the knowledge how harmonious and peaceful life can be. These recollections surface from the depths of their consciousness, and plunge the

Hakomies into despair and dark depression.

Perhaps it's the loss of hope, together with the expectation of salvation after death. Perhaps it's the lack of self-respect and the absence of joy in their life, or it may be a pathological alteration affecting their psyche and spirits. At all events, the Hakomies decide to commit collective suicide.

Only Pavati vigorously opposes their intention. But her influence has run out, like sand sifting through your fingers.

Can the tribe of the Hakomies – this peace-loving, harmonious, happy, joyful aspect of the great Whole – be allowed to disappear? Should their wisdom, their positive aura, their history, their special features and uniqueness be extinguished for ever? This people has been the darling of destiny for so long.

They have been the favorites of the gods! So what has changed? Are the gods angry, or are they asleep?

Pavati decides to wake the gods, to call on the All-One! She resolves to dance the dance of death.

A great fire is kindled on a hill, with sagebrush, birch and juniper wood. She dances around the fire and cries:

"The cosmic river has torn the bank away.
We are carried into the unknown, clinging to branches.
Fear and hopelessness blot out strength and reason.
Beings of the elements,
guardians and preservers,
flames of clarity,
here stand your children.

"We have let ourselves be devoured,
we have let ourselves be frozen,
we have let ourselves be drowned.

"We call out with our lives!
Give us certainty,
give us truth,
give us peace!"

Then Pavati makes an incision in her veins, and spurts the blood into the fire.

The sky darkens. Dragons – the guardians of treasure, guardians of the threshold – appear in the clouds, in the air and in the trees and bushes.

The Sakiras and the Hakomies, who by this time have been attracted by the smoke of the fire and come pouring onto the hill, freeze in terror. Finally the Hakomies recover from their petrifaction, emerge from the crowd and approach Pavati. All the members of the tribe are present. They are convinced that the time has come for their mass suicide – the end of the Hakomies.

Then the dragons rush in, picking up one Hakomie after another, and fly away. Even Pavati, who has now fallen unconscious to the ground, is rescued. The dragons fly with their burden far across the land, crossing valleys and mountain ranges, until they land on the roof of a massive temple located on the a mountain summit.

Two beautiful fairies, two fauns and a centaur are waiting as a reception committee. The Hakomies are brought down and led through a hall. Meanwhile the centaur looks after Pavati.

The hall is vast. It encloses a park with trees, meadows and shrubs. Birds can be heard twittering, and there is a gorgeous scent of flowers. In the center of the park is a beautiful fountain in the form of a giant water lily. Everything sparkles and glitters as if it is made of gold, crystal and precious stones. A cheerful, peaceful feeling pervades the hall. Some Hakomies think: "This must be paradise." Alongside the fountain, tables have been set up. The visitors hold their breath when they see there are just as many tables provided as in their village! Their hearts beat high, and past memories come to their minds . Instinctively they sit down at the tables, giving one another awkward looks. Deep sadness comes over them. Only when the centaur arrives with Pavati, who is still very weak, but otherwise clearly OK, are they stirred from their depression. Pavati grins all over her face, and nods encouragingly to the others.

In what always used to be Alo's place, the centaur now stands erect and speaks in a strong voice: "You summoned us! What do you need?"

The Hakomies excitedly tell the story of their having been captured and enslaved. They recount their terrible fate, their loss of hope of ever regaining freedom and independence. The centaur listens to the whole story with surprise, but without impatience. Then he asks some fairies to join him for a consultation.

The fairies bring cups and fill them with water from the fountain. Each of the Hakomies gets a full glass.

"This is the water of letting go," says one of the fairies. "Anyone who drinks it will see everything that caused them fear and trouble in the past with different eyes. They will strip off any supposed obligations, tasks, commandments and prohibitions, rituals, patterns of action, preventive and protective measures, insights, articles of faith, dreams and targets. No longer will anything seem important or significant. These are all illusions, colored air balloons, feelings and stories which our reason invents to distract us from the truth. You live in a fantasy world. Drink, and the thousand thoughts which tell you who and what you are, who you have to be and what you should do, will come to an end! You will only be able to see that which is."

A little nervously, the Hakomies drain their cups. Indeed, their bodies feel unbelievably light, almost free of gravity – as if all this time they had been carrying a heavy load on their shoulders, pressing down the whole body. A burden that simply falls away. Strength that was needed in the past to hold up and sustain these pressures has now been released. Everything is light, positively weightless.

The Hakomies look at each other in disbelief. Their astonishment becomes even greater when the ceiling of the gigantic hall starts to dissolve. At first it becomes transparent, and eventually it disappears entirely. Likewise the walls, the trees, the fountain, the whole park, the fairies and the other beings – they all dissolve into thin air. Only the Hakomies remain, standing on a vast mountain plateau. Cold wind whispers over their skin. The air is impregnated with a multitude of different scents which rise from the valley. The warmth of the sun feels good and penetrates them to a deep level. The colors of the sky and the landscape are unbelievably radiant and intense. It feels as if they have been living all this time under a bell jar or glass dome, which has now been taken away for the first time in their lives. For the first time the Hakomies perceive the surrounding world as it is in truth, unfiltered and directly, without insulating layers.

The feeling of the moment, of the plants and animals, of the mountain plateau, of the entire world is tangibly present. The sense of happiness is so overwhelming, the moment so fascinating, that their thoughts, even the unconscious ones, simply come to a stop. There is nothing left that could ever be more important than this moment. There is nothing left to want or wish for. There is no time any more, no past and no future, no cause and effect. Only this perfect state – of just being here – just being.

No one can say how long the Hakomies remain in this happily floating state. At some point, perhaps actually right from the beginning, several invisible but clearly perceptible beings appear. Perhaps it is a dimension of consciousness which has always been there but is only now being perceived. This dimension, or this aspect of space, removes the gray haze from their sluggish and laboring brains. The Hakomies can now grasp even complicated logical relations and causal connections effortlessly and with playful ease, and follow lines of thought calling for concentration and effort without a problem. Their thoughts are razor-sharp and as clear as mountain lakes, as clear as glass. It's as if each one of them has been connected to a very much higher intelligence. Suddenly it is perfectly obvious who has done what and why, what was the background, the cause and the meaning of all the events they have experienced. Whatever question comes into their mind, immediately there follow the moment of revelation. Chandeliers radiate with breathtaking brightness. The world seems simply structured, clear and perfect. Everything makes sense, it all coheres. Everything is necessary and important. It all forms part of a perfect system.

The being or dimension, or whatever it is, becomes increasingly concrete and more tangible, but remains pure consciousness, and speaks with a mighty voice which is not perceived with the ears but felt through the entire body:

"See who you really are."

Behind the group, the entrance to a cave appears. Each of the group goes into the cave alone.

What follows, dear reader, is only intended as an example. It is one story out of the reservoir of infinite possibilities. Your story undoubtedly looks different. More probable, more reasonable, more normal perhaps. Your story relates how you are living now, how you have lived and will live in future. What follows is the story of Igasho. Igasho is one of the fishermen who were sent out to explore the mainland.

Igasho enters the cave. When his eyes get used to the darkness, he can see a light glimmering in the distance. Nothing can be seen or heard of the others. He is alone.

While he walks toward the light, he notices that his appearance is changing. He looks down at himself, finds himself strange and yet somehow at the same time familiar. As if he were someone else, but someone he has known for a long time. Finally he arrives in a room lit with diffuse light. A chair and a table are before him. Not a sound can be heard. It is absolutely still.

As if it were the most natural thing in the world, he sits down on the chair and opens the book lying on the table, with the familiar feeling of having done this thousands and thousands of times before. He reads the most recent entries. Entries written in his own handwriting – evidently he has written them himself.

They give a detailed report of his external appearance, his thoughts, his character, his emotions, his actions and his experiences. Surprised and incredulous, he realizes that his entire being and entire life have been written down by himself in this book. Without a second thought he picks up the pen, and continues writing the story:

"Pavati stands with her opened veins in front of the fire. I am horrified, positively frozen. My blood pounds in my head and ears. My understanding is fogged, and only one thought struggles up to the surface: Have I got to do this now? We all of us wanted to kill ourselves! I'm frightened. What if I'm the sole survivor? How bad will my punishment be? I'm afraid! I feel sick. Behind me I hear clattering and cries. My paralysis melts – I turn around and see the Sakira warriors. They are armed, and marching up the hill. Somehow I feel relief. Now at least this frightful situation and the unbearable inner conflict will be resolved. I can't do anything – I don't need to do anything now. The warriors will determine what happens next. Fate has decided. I don't have to kill myself."

Igasho gets up, puts on a costume and assumes the form known to him as Igasho before. He leaves the room, and a few meters further on comes to a stage. On the stage some of his tribe are gathered, likewise clad in "costumes". Pavati too is present. At the edge of the stage, the "actors" disguised as Sakira warriors are waiting for their cue.

The play begins. Igasho acts out exactly what he has previously written. The others likewise play out the gestures and roles they have imagined for themselves. The plot unfolds. One of the warriors kills a Hakomie with a martial yell. The performance breaks off, they all hasten back to their tables and write frantically about how they are going to go on from here. What is their judgment of the deed? How should they respond?

The dead Hakomie leaves the stage, writes a moving funeral scene and starts a new story. It begins with the birth of an enchantingly beautiful baby in a strange country. In this new life, his parents treat him lovingly and are affluent. He has new tasks, new abilities, a new character and new chances of development.

Igasho sits over his book and is confused. It becomes clear to him that he – not the role he is playing as Igasho, but he himself – is the author of his life. That he has the freedom to write anything he can make happen on the stage, if that is what he wants. Of course the others are writing their own stories and playing out their own scripts. His script is in his own hands and no one else's. No one compels him to present the same character his whole life long, to identify with the same values, always to react in the same way to similar situations or to meet his own expectations or those of others. The supposed compulsions are his own inventions. He compels himself, because he believes in this way he can prevent certain consequences or must avoid them. But are the consequences he expects really compulsory?

He is free, after all, and shouldn't be making his decisions dependent on suppositions and articles of faith. We can't know how a thing is going to turn out. The world is too complex for that. We can only listen to our hearts, and choose from the possible courses of action with maximum attentiveness. Our choice is not limited by circumstances, but by our creativity and our fear.

Igasho decides to change it all. He goes back on the stage. Some actors have already begun to fight. He stands in front of Pavati, who is now lying lifeless on the ground, and shouts with all his might, "Stop! Stop it at once!" To his great surprise, though he has always been an anxious kind of person, he now feels completely relaxed, sure of himself and confident of his power. His cry is so penetrating, that the fighting actually comes to a stop.

Everyone turns to him expectantly. He looks into tense and anxious faces. Even the faces of the Sakira warriors show uncertainty, self-doubt and fear.

He calls: "Pavati died for us, to invoke the gods and get justice for us! Sakiras, your punishment will be terrible! Your wealth will disappear, sickness will torment you, you are marked for death!"

The eyes of the Sakiras, and their fear, get bigger all the time. Of course Igasho knows that all this cannot be brought about by him or by Pavati. But it chimes in with the logic and the fears of the Sakiras. They see this prophecy as absolutely convincing. They will unconsciously act in such a way that the prophecy finds fulfillment, in order to uphold their picture of the world.

Igasho continues: "There is only one way for you to appease the wrath of the gods. End our slavery and give us freedom. Give the Hakomies the same rights you enjoy. If you kill us, you annihilate yourselves. You have the power to decide, and you have the responsibility for what happens. We don't need to fight."

Igasho leaves the stage, well pleased. This was a scene that would never, even remotely, have been in keeping with his old personality. All the same, he hasn't been killed, or laughed out of court. Gradually he gets a sense of what all this must mean: love, hate, pain, joy, happiness, honesty and lies – they are all just fabulous theater.

Igasho goes back on stage. Not to take part in the play, but to take a closer look at the actors and see what is happening in the wings.

The beings behind the masks are similar to him. Some are still young and have little experience. Some are old, with many lives and many experiences behind them. Almost all of them are so heavily identified with their roles that they have forgotten who they really are. They think the masks and disguises are their true appearance, confusing their story with their true life, and their articles of faith with their true character. In childhood they adopted the wishes, values, anxieties and mistaken estimates of their parents. They have forgotten truth, and forgotten themselves. As adults, they look for acknowledgement and affluence. No time is left for them to seek the truth behind the illusion, to discover the real player.

A gong resounds, and Igasho is standing on the mountain again, alone. The wind blows in his face. He is is still perceiving his surroundings without any filter, without any kind of boundaries. Then he sees the fountain from which he drank the water. Instinctively, without thinking about it, he gets into the fountain. As he enters the water, his body starts to dissolve, as if he were made of salt. First his hands disappear, then his arms and legs. Finally he dissolves completely. But this is not painful, or associated with any unpleasant feeling. On the contrary, he doesn't really disappear, he just disperses himself in the water. The water is no longer around him, he is in it. He is the water. His self extends into the surrounding environment and melts into it.

The water evaporates, and he goes with it. He expands into the air, into the clouds and over the entire world. He is a part of the entire planet, of all animals, all plants, all intelligent living creatures, all seas, lakes, mountains, stones and everything else. All is a part of him, of his consciousness, and his consciousness is in everything. Every living creature, every object, he perceives as if it were himself. He has been dissolved in the great All. Now the whole truth shines on him.

The planet, with all that happens on it, is a perfect system. It is unimportant whether I am the torturer or the tortured, whether I eat or am eaten, whether I am perpetrator or victim. All are just sides of the same medal, all are just paths. Paths inviting me to make decisions.

I myself judge and choose who and what I am. If I appear to have no choice, no alternative, this is because I am willfully blinding myself, tying myself down or because I am too fearful to choose. The system always permits you to make a choice. Using this chance is my choice as well.

What a gift… It is completely selfless, without any obligation, without intention, without calling for any counterperformance, all just out of love.

The fairies surround the fountain, and draw Igasho's awareness and feeling of happiness and contentment back into the circle. With breathtaking speed, his consciousness collects and concentrates itself once more in the body floating in the fountain. He comes back to the here and now.

He and the other members of the group get out of the fountain one by one. They find themselves again in the roofed park where the journey began, and beam at each other with happy faces, still out of themselves. No one speaks. Some giggle quietly.

The dragons bring the Hakomies back to the hill where it all started. In the eyes of the advancing Sakira warriors, the scene that enacts itself is a miracle. Pavati, who is lying on the ground, suddenly gets up and is completely OK. The Hakomies, who were fearful before, are suddenly quietly happy. They radiate power and contentment. They really seem to be shining.

For the Sakiras, there is only one explanation: Pavati is a mighty enchantress who is in league with a higher power. They believe that the the Hakomies are protected and watched over by spirits or some divinity. The sudden change in the slaves, the happenings around the fire, the darkened skies have made the Sakiras very nervous. They remember all too well what they have done to the Hakomies. For fear of worse happening, they give them their freedom.

The Hakomies separate and go in all directions of the compass. They adapt to the customs of the various tribes and peoples they go among, and live as healers, counselors, teachers or as simple farmers. Each one lives one life, each follows one path. But this time no one chooses pain. Always at four in the morning, they wake up and get in contact with each other telepathically.

Maybe you too will meet somebody who meditates at four in the morning. If his presence seems to light up the room, you have probably come across a Hakomie

Water droplet

High in the sky, in the clouds, a water droplet comes into the world. Mist is its mother, its father an icy air current. "Gee, this is great!" the water drop exults. Up and down it floats in its father's storms and its mother's towers and pinnacles of cloud, along with thousands of its brothers and sisters. Wilder and wilder grows the helter-skelter ride, and the drops squeak and yodel with excitement.

Suddenly it senses a change. Mother and father aren't around any more. They are still there, but he is no longer in them. The wild up and down movement has disappeared. The only movement now is in one direction, monotonous and weightless. The droplet feels anxious. Gravity, which gave him orientation, is gone, and his parents are speeding away into the distance. He and his thousands of brother and sister water drops screech frantically, "Mother, father, hold me! I'm falling!" But who can stop the rain from falling?

Father gives it his best shot. He blows and storms for all he is worth, to brake the fall of his children, to save them. But in vain! His forces only succeed in distorting the droplets. The original perfection of their spherical form is stretched, pulled out of line and what remains are deformed misshapen droplets. Some even freeze into ice.

Their fear escalates into panic. There's something unknown coming, something none of them has ever seen, and it's coming to meet them. A colored, strangely shaped and hard-looking expanse which extends from horizon to horizon. All attempts at evading it are fruitless. The crash is inevitable. As if from a deep cellar vault, deathly fear rises like a bogeyman in their minds. "We're going to hell!" shrieks the droplet, and the air is getting warmer all the time. At breathtaking speed, he splashes down…

At some point he recovers consciousness and finds – miraculously – that he isn't dead. On the contrary, for some mysterious reason he feels snug as a bug in a rug.

"Where am I?" he calls. All around him, thousands and thousands of drops are calling out in the same way. Gradually he realizes that he and his many brothers and sisters have landed in a hollow and formed a puddle. He isn't alone.

This happy state doesn't last long – then he feels movement again at the heart of his being. Slowly but steadily, he and his siblings start to flow. They flow through small channels, passing entities who call themselves plants, passing hard stones, and something tickles his belly that is called earth.

The plants whisper: "Come to me and become like me! I grow toward the sun, unfold my leaves and blossom into beauty. Join with me and I'll carry you into the highest branches of my being."

The earth sings: "Join with me! I'll mingle with you and we'll make mud – mud that warms, covers everything, fills everything. With me you will become an unconquerable viscous mass. I promise you the protection and shelter of mother earth."

Only the stone screeches: "Keep away from me! I hate everything that wants to change me. You want to polish me and hollow me out? I'm staying hard. No way leads to me, you can only go by."

The water droplet isn't impressed by these threats and seductions. He goes on flowing, and joins with more and more of his brothers and sisters. Then he, and with him all the other drops, has a worrying thought: "Where's it all going? What am I turning into? What is going to become of me?" He mourns for his past – when he was still a free floating droplet in Mother Cloud. "Back then I wasn't afraid of the future, because there wasn't a future, there was only Now. I was sure that I would always be a perfect round drop and would always be gently sustained. Now everything's changing, and I'm changing as well. Who and what I am depends now on my surroundings and the forces affecting me. Of myself I have no fixed boundaries, no fixed form. I flow. How can I cope with the future, without a boundary or form of my own? Do I have any influence on the future? Who or what am I, without a fixed form?"

119

The water drop starts to weep bitterly. Of course no one can see the tears, which are immediately reabsorbed. That makes him even sadder and lonelier.

The weeping drops form a stream and flow down the mountain. Whenever they have to avoid a stone, their whispered laments can be heard. They complain that they always have to change, that they are constantly forced to seek new paths. They would so like to be stone with set boundaries, hard to the core. Then others would have to get out of the way. But in a hundred years' time they would still be the same. But what is going to become of a formless droplet?

The stream flows into a lake. The lake lies calm and majestic in its valley, holding up its mirror in the sun to the sky, the clouds and the mountains. In a deep voice it admonishes the drops: "Why are you afraid of the future and your own impermanence? I consist of millions of drops, and have already existed for a thousand years. I will always exist, and you will exist along with me. So be quiet, just enjoy the beauty and the tranquility."

The droplet, and the others with him, don't dare to complain out loud, but they think: "Beauty? Doesn't that call for a form as well? Will I ever be beautiful? The lake only has its form because we drops, who make up the lake, are without a form of our own. It exists, because we flow into it. But where does that leave me? I want to reflect majestic clouds too. I want to be admired for my beauty too. I don't just want to be part of a lake."

Hardly has the water drop thought this thought through, when a shadow swoops over the lake. A bird plunges into the water, snapping at fishes. It swallows the drop along with a fish. The drop is dispersed in the body of the bird and becomes a part of it. The drop becomes bird.

He is delighted: "At last I am somebody! At last I have a form!" Joyfully he greets all the other drops, cells, molecules and various substances which – in close partnership, with great enthusiasm and loving commitment – make up the bird and keep it alive. Being integrated in this system is hard work. He has to perform important tasks, and function in accordance with precise rules. But the reward for this cooperation – a wonderful being that can fly, that gleams gloriously in the sun with its beautiful shimmering colors – is enough to make up for all the effort. A miracle of nature – his new "I", his new home. Now he has a form and a foreseeable future. He can even visit Mother Cloud and Father Wind sometimes, and feel them all around him. Not quite in the same way as before, for there are feathers and many other substances in between, but his parents are quite close, and Father Wind lets him dance for joy and hover weightlessly.

In the course of time the drop forgets that he is a drop. He starts to think and act like a bird. He even begins to strive for a bird's goals. He lives a bird's life. The illusion that he is the creature itself becomes a conviction. Without him, the creature wouldn't exist. What a massive mistake!

When the time comes, he is excreted from the bird.

It's an extremely painful feeling, no longer being form, no longer being bird. He's lost his identity. The illusion has been vaporized by the truth, just as the droplet himself now evaporates in the heat of the sun. The moisture rises and becomes reunited with Mother Cloud.

Mother and father give birth to the droplet yet again and release him into the world. By circuitous routes and transformations of mist into ice and water, the droplet flows into a body. This time it's a human body.

Basically the human body functions in a very similar way to the bird's body. But there's a special feature – the person thinks, just as the drop used to, that he is something intrinsic, that he has a form, a form with which he is totally identified. All too well, the droplet remembers the illusion. He still feels the pain of the loss. The human being, on the other hand, has long since forgotten the time when he was formless. He is deaf to the drop's experiences. Nor does he see that he is just the result of many drops, cells, molecules and other substances which interact. He thinks he is an identity of his own. But eventually his time is come, and the world excretes him. This is the time of dissolution, the time of flowing.

I am not the form, and yet I am.
I am conscious being,
which lives in matter and in movement.
Forms are illusions.
True is only the imperishable.…
the storm,
the rain,
the elements,
the interaction
and the flowing.
That is what we really are and always will be.

The author and the artist

Bernd Strohmeyer, born in 1961, lives in Bernau on Lake Chiemsee, in Bavaria, Germany. At the age of fifty he gave up his banking career in favor of psychotherapy. He trained in hypnosis and in humanistic and systemic methods of therapy, is the author of many fairytales and short stories with a psychological background. He works as a counselor.

Marah Strohmeyer-Haider also lives on Lake Chiemsee. She works as an art and design therapist. For many years she has been active as an artist, course coordinator and networker.

Recommended books

Der verborgene Tempel: Eine Innenreise von der Spaltung zur Einheit [The Hidden Temple: an Inner Journey from Division to Unity] (cloth binding)

"The more we veil ourselves, the bigger our shadow becomes."

This unusual book invites the reader to join in experiencing an adventure – to enter on a journey where valuable discoveries can be made.

What prevents people from leading a fulfilled life? What causes feelings of inferiority, conflicts and crises?

Three different paths lead to the "hidden temple", and so to overcoming inner and outer divisions and finding harmony with oneself and with the world. The first path is a life history. Realistic and symbolic at once, it pursues dramatic twists and turns, where the reader is given space to find him- or herself in the mirror of the story. It is the story of one who is confronted with destructive powers in another world, and comes to earth in order to learn. The second path consists in resonant pictures by Marah Strohmeyer-Haider, which encourage the reader to engage sensuously with the questions of existence. Finally a diary documents the steps by which the seeker gradually becomes more conscious, until the point is reached where he or she can reconcile with him- or herself. This report draws on psychotherapeutic and systemic approaches, summarizes the experiences of the life journey and explains the background from a spiritual point of view.

The book helps us to get our bearings in the world. Solutions become possible, so we can live in love as self-determining beings. It shows how close we are to unity.

Clothbound edition: 128 pages
Published by Books on Demand. 1st edition, 2 February 2017
Language: German
ISBN-10: 374317832X
ISBN-13: 978-3743178328
Measurements: 19.5 x 1.7 x 27.7 cm

Zusammenspiel: Eine karmische Reise [Interplay: a Karmic Journey]
(paperback)

Apparently it all starts with the slaughterhouse worker Helfried deciding, from  one day to the next, to give up his job. He can't explain it to himself, and wants to find out what is going on with his life. His search takes him and a female traveling companion on an adventurous journey to Tibet, where he gains clarity from a meeting with a monk and experiences a liberating transformation. But the story actually started much earlier, in a farmhouse, with a young couple, a long time ago – and perhaps goes back even farther… People keep acting in accordance with unconscious patterns, and they and others then have to suffer the unfortunate consequences. On his journey Helfried becomes able to recognize such patterns of behavior and grow beyond them, by perceiving himself in other people and their life stories. At the same time this book encourages those who read it like a mandala, a meditative picture, to reflect, points them in the direction of existential questions and inspires them to find helpful answers.

Paperback edition: 88 pages
Published by Books on Demand. 1st edition, 20 March 2017
Language: German
ISBN-10: 3743187736
ISBN-13: 978-3743187733
Measurements: 12.7 x 0.5 x 20.3 cm